Acclaim for
Zalacaín the Adventurer

"In 1956, Ernest Hemingway visited the dying Spanish author Baroja and told him that the Nobel Prize Hemingway had recently won rightfully belonged to Baroja. This fast-moving novel of youthful exuberance, set in the Basque country of Spain during the last Carlist wars (1872–1876), features the shenanigans of the closet liberal Zalacaín. [He] emerges as a hero unbound by convention, who pushes his destiny to the limit, often escaping from his predicaments only in the 11th hour and becoming successful as a Carlist agent, smuggler, kidnapper of nuns, and lover of many women. This novel requires an understanding of a time and place not well known to Americans, and Diendl does an admirable job of providing it."

—*Library Journal*

"Anyone should like *Zalacaín the Adventurer* by Pio Baroja, a classical Spanish writer of the 1890s. His popular work has been translated into English by James Diendl who has taught at Ohio State University, Miami University, and Mount Union College. Zalacaín combines the footloose childhood of a Tom Sawyer with the street savvy of an incorrigible teen truant. He fools everyone, has fun with his comrades and female friends, and miraculously survives all hazards in achieving his monetary and amatory goals."

—*Akron Beacon Journal*

Zalacaín
the
Adventurer

The History of the Good Fortune
and Wanderings of
Martin Zalacaín of Urbia

Pío Baroja

Translated and with an Introduction by
James P. Diendl

LOST
COAST
PRESS

ZALACAÍN THE ADVENTURER
A History of the Good Fortune and Wanderings
of Martin Zalacaín of Urbia by Pío Baroja

For information, phone (707) 964-9520. For bookseller and library discounts or credit card orders, please call 800-883-7782. Or write to:

Lost Coast Press
155 Cypress Street
Fort Bragg CA 95437

PUBLISHERS CATALOGING-IN-PUBLICATION

Baroja, Pio, 18721956.
Zalacaín the adventurer: A history of the good fortune and wanderings of Martin Zalacaín of Urbia / by Pío Baroja ; translated and with an introduction by James P. Diendl. 1st ed.
p. cm.
Preassigned LCCN 97-73593
Print: ISBN 10 1-882897-13-7
        ISBN 13 978-1-882897-13-1
Ebook: ISBN 978-1-935448-21-1
Audio book: ISBN 978-1-60031-005-8
1. Spain History Carlist War, 18731876 Fiction.I. Diendl, James P.II. Title.

PQ6603.A7Z35 1997863.62
QBI97-40841

Cover design by Colored Horse Studios
Cover illustration: "No. 5 And They Are Like Wild Beasts", from *Disasters of War*, Goya. Copyright 1995, Zedcor, Inc., Tucson, Az.

PRINTED IN THE UNITED STATES OF AMERICA

First Edition
3 5 7 9 10 8 6 4 2

Note To the Reader

IN TRANSLATING THIS NOVEL I have attempted to stay as close and faithful as possible to the author's grammatical and syntactical style. Sometimes this style may seem complex, but my intent was to give the reader a feel for Baroja's personal literary style as well as that of the period in which he wrote.

James P. Diendl

Contents

Zalacaín
the
Adventurer

Introduction

MARTIN ZALACAÍN, THE HERO of Pío Baroja's novel *Zalacaín the Adventurer,* is a restless, courageous young man seeking fulfillment in a world of chaos and brutality. He realizes the basic absurdity of the civil war in which he gets involved, but faces it as a personal challenge. For Martin, inactivity is equivalent to death, and war becomes the vehicle for the heroic exploits that give meaning to his life. He is never satisfied; each feat he accomplishes leads to one more daring. The story of Martin Zalacaín is universal in its portrayal of man's perpetual quest for adventure and of youth's search for a meaningful existence. But to fully appreciate this novel the reader must be aware of its historical background.

During the nineteenth century Spain experienced a series of costly wars, frequent changes of government, and general unrest. The century opened with Spain's involvement in the Napoleonic Wars and Napoleon's invasion of the country in 1808, initiating the Spanish War of Independence, which lasted until 1814; it closed with the humiliating and disastrous defeat in the Spanish-American War of 1898.

Between these two catastrophic events several wars were waged over succession rights to the throne. In 1814, after the fall of Napoleon, Ferdinand VII became king and ruled tyrannically until his death in 1833. In that year Ferdinand's daughter, a child at the time, was proclaimed Queen Isabella II. However, Ferdinand's brother, Charles, contested Isabella's claim to the throne and thus began the first of the Carlist Civil Wars of the nineteenth century.

The first full-scale Carlist War (1833–39) ended in the defeat of the pretender's cause with the Convention of Vergara in 1839. Isabella's mother, Maria Cristina, was regent during this period, and she was

1

forced to solicit the aid of liberals since the conservative, traditionalist elements were supporting the claim of Charles. But even though the Carlists suffered defeat the cause never died. When Isabella came to power she proved to be morally irresponsible, and in 1868 she was ultimately dethroned. In 1870 an Italian, Amadeo of Savoy, accepted the offer of the throne but reigned only until 1873 when he abdicated. During Amadeo's reign the second and last major Carlist War (1872–76) began.

The original pretender's eldest son, also named Charles, had taken over his father's claim in 1845, and was in turn succeeded in 1861 by his younger brother John. In 1868 John abdicated in favor of his eldest son who was proclaimed King Charles VII by his followers. Four years later the Carlist War was renewed, this time directed against Amadeo. Following Amadeo's abdication Spain was proclaimed a republic, which lasted only until 1874 when the Bourbon dynasty was restored with the coronation of Alphonse XII, son of Isabella II. King Alphonse finally succeeded in ending the Carlist War in 1876.

This, then, is the historical background of Baroja's novel, *Zalacaín the Adventurer*. The story takes place mainly during the last of the Carlist wars (1872–76). The setting for the adventure is primarily the Basque region of Spain, located in the north, in the western area of the Pyrenees. The Basque territories in Spain include the provinces of Navarre, Álava, Guipúzcoa, and Biscay. The French-Basque territories in the *département* of Basses-Pyrenees are Basse-Navarre, Labourd, and Soule.

Basques are energetic, individualistic people who have traditionally been staunch Catholics. The pretender, Charles, and his successors, received strong support from the Basque regions because of the religious fanaticism associated with his movement and because Charles opposed the attempts by the liberals to encroach upon local privileges in these provinces. The Basques have always held tenaciously to their *fueros*— laws granting provincial rights and privileges. Even in very recent times Basque separatist movements have caused problems for the Spanish government.

The Basques speak their own language. Although it is known that

Introduction

Basque does not belong to the Indo-European family, the precise origin of this language is still a mystery. Today, however, most Basques speak Spanish or French.

The author of *Zalacaín the Adventurer,* Pío Baroja y Nessi, was born in San Sebastian in the Basque province of Guipúzcoa on December 28, 1872, the year in which the last Carlist War began. He died in Madrid on October 30, 1956. Baroja is certainly one of the best Spanish novelists of the twentieth century. He is the foremost novelist of the Generation of 1898, a group of highly creative, individualistic, concerned Spanish writers who succeeded in infusing new life into their literature. The term was popularized by Azorín, pseudonym of José Martínez Ruiz, one of its most prominent members. The year 1898 was, of course, a significant one in Spanish history because it marked the culmination of the decadence that had begun back in the sixteenth century. The writers of Baroja's generation, although individualistic, were nevertheless united in their dissatisfaction with the situation then existing in their country.

The Generation of 1898 is, therefore, not a genuine literary movement but rather a term that characterizes the spirit of an era whose writers displayed their sincere concern for their country's present and future and who sought to revive some of the past glory. In addition to Baroja and Azorín, the group includes Miguel de Unamuno, Ramón María del Valle-Inclán, Antonio Machado, Juan Ramón Jiménez, and Jacinto Benavente.

Although Baroja revealed his typical Basque individualism by denying his membership in the Generation of 1898, or in any other group for that matter, his pessimism, critical attitude and concern for his country are characteristic also of his contemporaries. Baroja studied medicine and worked as a doctor for a few years in a small town in his native Basque country. He soon became disillusioned with that life and went to Madrid to operate a bakery. Finding no success in that venture either, he decided to try writing. At last he had found his forte: he succeeded in selling his articles to the Madrid newspapers and published his first book in 1900. Among Baroja's literary favorites were Poe, Dickens, Balzac, and Dostoevsky. But again, in regard to his novels, Baroja was a unique

3

individualist. He was a very productive author, with approximately one hundred literary works to his credit. His early novels were regional, set in the Basque provinces. He arranged many of the novels written in his youth in trilogies. In the trilogy *The Struggle for Life,* Baroja deals with the Madrid proletariat and displays his anarchistic tendencies. And in the trilogy *The Fanciful Life,* the author describes the struggles through life of the characters Silvester Paradox and Ferdinand Ossorio with auto-biographical touches. *Memoirs of a Man of Action* is the general title of a series of historical or semi-historical novels, similar in scope and treatment at least, to the *National Episodes* of Pérez Galdós.

In the novels of Baroja, plot and characterization always take second place to action. The author himself, however, was not a man of action but rather a reflective man who wrote about men of action. Thus, in his works we usually find a conflict between action and reflection. Martin Zalacaín is a fine example of Baroja's man of action; he has an insatiable appetite for it as he reveals near the end of the novel:

> *"What do you expect?*
> *I grew up wild like the grass and*
> *I need action, continuous action."*

There is a strong picaresque strain evident in most of Baroja's work. We can certainly see this in the character of Martin Zalacaín as he struggles to overcome the numerous obstacles confronting him in his efforts to make something of his life. Along with the picaresque quality, Baroja's novels contain many episodic and anecdotal interludes. The plot is never contrived; things happen in his novels as they do in life — in a desultory, unpredictable fashion. But because of the accent on action, Baroja's novels are fast-moving and easy to read. The pessimistic note is usually apparent but often counterbalanced by a satirical humor.

Zalacaín the Adventurer is, then, a regional novel with a strong historical background. It appeared in 1909 as the third novel of the trilogy, *Basque Land.* It is lighter in tone than the two preceding novels of the trilogy, *The House of Aizgorri* (1900), a novel in dramatic form on life in a Basque village, and *The Eldest Son of Labraz* (1903), a pessimistic novel of Basque country life that presents the story of two unscrupulous characters.

Zalacaín the Adventurer has always been one of Baroja's most popular novels, probably because the pessimistic mood does not prevail here and because of the youthful exuberance with which it abounds. It is definitely one of the author's most entertaining and enjoyable works.

James P. Diendl
Mount Union College

Prologue

What the Town of Urbia Was Like in the Last Third of the Nineteenth Century

URBIA IS SURROUNDED BY a high, black wall of stone. This wall continues along the highway, bounds the town on the north, and when it reaches the river it twists and bisects the church, leaving part of the presbytery out of its circumference, and then scales a summit and encloses the city on the south.

In the fosses one still sees puddle-marked terrain with weeds and posterns full of shackles, cut-off sentry boxes, moss-covered stepladders; all around, on the slopes facing the fortification, are tall and romantic groves, thickets and clusters of trees, and green meadows dotted with little flowers. Nearby on the steep hill at the foot of which the town rests, a somber castle hides amidst gigantic elm trees.

From the highway Urbia appears as a cluster of decrepit, decayed, sloping houses, with overhanging wooden balconies and belvederes that peep over the black stone wall which surrounds them.

Urbia is divided into two districts—the old and the new. The old one, the "street," as it is called by antonomasia in Basque, is primarily formed by two narrow, winding little streets on a slope which merge in the square.

From the road of the old town one can view a broken line of oblique and dirty roofs which gradually descends from the castle to the river. The houses, elevated within the stone belt of the city, seem at first sight to be in a rigid and uncomfortable position; however, just the contrary is true because between the foot of the houses and the fortified walls there is a huge space occupied by a series of magnificent orchards. These orchards, protected from the cold winds, are excellent. In them they can cultivate tropic-zone plants such as orange and lemon trees.

On the inside part of the wall which faces the orchards there is a path formed by large slabs, a kind of sidewalk, a little more than a yard wide with its iron balustrade.

In the interstices of these old and rain-corroded slabs grow the poisonous cicuta and the henbane; next to the walls, in the spring, shine the yellowish flowers of the dandelion and the verbascum, the gladioli of beautiful crimson color, and the purple foxgloves. Many other weeds, mixed with nettles and poppies, extend along the wall and adorn with their verdure and their constellations of small and simple flowers the merlons, the crenels, and the machicolation galleries.

During the winter, in the daytime, some old people of the neighborhood, in robes and slippers, walk along the cornice, and when March or April comes, they contemplate the progress of the beautiful pear and peach trees of the orchards.

They also secretly look through the crenels to see if some coach or cart is coming to town, if there is anything new in the houses of the new district; not without a certain hostility, because all the inhabitants of the inner city feel an obscure and inexplicable antipathy for their neighbors who live on the other side of the walls.

Several ogival gates adorn the stone belt of the old town in some places; in other places the wall is broken irregularly, leaving a gap which seems to increase every day.

On some of the gates, under the old pointed arch, there is a half ogival arch subsequently made for some unknown reason.

Shackles for the posterns remain embedded in the stones of the jambs. Drawbridges are replaced by piles of earth that fill up the foss to the necessary height.

Urbia offers various aspects, according to the place from which it is contemplated; from a distance and coming from the road, especially at dusk, it has the appearance of a feudal castle: the fortress, somber, surrounded by large trees and prolonged then by the town with its fortified walls, which spout water, presents an austere and warlike aspect; on the other hand, from the bridge on a sunny day, Urbia does not give any sullen impression; on the contrary, it seems a diminutive Florence, settled on the banks of a clear, stony, rippling little stream with a rapid current.

The two rows of houses bathed by the river are old houses with blackish galleries and belvederes, on which hang laundry put out to dry and strings of garlic and peppers. These galleries have at one end a pulley and a wooden pail for hoisting up water. When the houses end, following the banks of the river, there are some orchards, along the greenish walls of which, tall, thin, and spiritual cypress trees rise up, and this gives to that remote place a greater Florentine aspect.

The city inside the walls ends quickly; besides the two long streets, there are only moist and narrow lanes and the square. The latter is a lugubrious intersection consisting of one of the walls of the church, with several wall gratings, of the City Hall, with its projecting balconies and its huge front door decorated with the towns coat of arms, and of an enormous house, where on the ground floor Azpillaga's store is located.

Azpillaga's store, where one can find everything, must give the villagers the impression of a Pandora's box, of an unexplored world full of marvels. At Azpillaga's front door, hanging from the black walls, one can usually see pelota rackets, packsaddles, halter headstalls, saddle trappings of Andalusian style, and in the windows, which serve as showcases, flasks of colored caramels, complicated fishing tackle, with red float and rods, nets fastened to a handle, tin frames, plaster and brass saints, and old stamps, which are dirty because of time and flies.

Inside there are clothes, blankets, wools, ham, bottles of adulterated chartreuse, fine china... The British Museum is nothing, in variety, next to this store.

Azpillaga, corpulent, majestic, with his clerical air, blue sleeves and his beret, usually paces at the door. The two main streets of Urbia are narrow, winding and sloping. Most of the residents of those two streets are farmers, sandal makers, and wagon carpenters. The farmers, in the morning, go out to the fields with their yokes. When the town wakes up at dawn, they hear the lowing of the oxen; then the sandal makers take their benches out to the sidewalk, and the carpenters work in the middle of the street in the company of little children, hens, and dogs.

Some of the houses of the two main streets show their coats of arms; others, maxims written in Latin, and the majority, a number, the date on which they were made and the name of the couple who had them built...

Today the town almost exclusively consists of the new, clean, pleasant, somewhat presumptuous part. In the summer an endless number of cars cross the highway, and almost all stop a while at the Ohando house, converted into the Grand Hotel of Urbia. Some young ladies, with a passion for the picturesque, while their fat daddy is writing postcards in the hotel, ascend the steps of the entrance to the old section. They follow a narrow and lugubrious crack in the wall, which goes down by means of a zigzag slope to the highway to survey the two main streets of the city and take photographs of the places that seem romantic to them and of the groups of sandal makers who allow themselves to be photographed, smiling mockingly.

Forty years ago, life in Urbia was calm and simple; on Sundays there was the event of high mass, and in the afternoon, the event of vespers. Later, the drummer would go to a meadow annexed to the fortress and claimed by the town and the people would dance gaily to the sound of the fife and the tabor, until the ringing of the Angelus would put an end to the merrymaking, and the villagers would return to their homes after making a stop at the tavern.

Part I

Zalacaín's Childhood

Chapter 1

How Martin Zalacaín
Lived and Was Educated

A SLOPING ROAD DESCENDS from the fortress, passes over the cemetery, and crosses the gate to France. This road, on the high part, has several stone crosses at the sides, and at the end of it there is a hermitage, and on the lower part, after entering the city, it becomes a street. On the left-hand side of the road, years ago before the wall, there was an old dwelling, half demolished, with its earthen roof full of rough pieces of stone and the sandy stone of its walls worn down by the action of the humidity and the air. On the front of the decrepit and poor house, a hole indicated where the coat of arms was placed in the past, and under it one could discern, rather than read, several letters that composed a Latin phrase: *"Post funera virtus vivit."*

In this house was born Martin Zalacaín of Urbia, who later was to be called Zalacaín the Adventurer, and he spent the early years of his childhood there; in this house he dreamed his first adventures and broke in his first pair of pants.

The Zalacaíns lived just a short distance from Urbia; but neither Martin nor his family were citizens: his house was located just a few yards outside of the town proper.

Martin's father was a farmer, a sullen man who talked very little and who died during a smallpox epidemic; Martin's parents had very little character; his mother lived in that psychological obscurity which is common among country people, and she was married and became a widow with total unconsciousness. When her husband died she was left with two children, Martin and a younger daughter named Ignacia.

The house in which the Zalacaíns lived belonged to the Ohando family, the oldest, most aristocratic, and richest family in Urbia.

Martin's mother practically lived on the charity of the Ohandos.

In such conditions of poverty and misery, it seemed logical that, through the combination of heredity and environment, Martin should be like his parents: sullen, timid, and cowardly; but the boy turned out to be determined, daring, and bold.

In this period, children did not go to school as much as they do now, and Martin attended school very irregularly. The only thing he knew about it was that it was a gloomy place, with a few white signs on the walls, which did not encourage him to enter. Another thing that kept him away from that modest center of learning was seeing that the children of the street did not accept him in their group because he lived outside the town and always went around looking like a tramp.

For this reason he felt hatred toward them; thus when some kids from the settlement beyond the walls entered the street and began a stone fight with the citizens, Martin was one of the most enraged in the combat; he led the fierce gangs, directed them and even dominated them. He had among the other children the power of his boldness and temerity. There was no place in town that Martin did not know. For him, Urbia was the gathering place of all beautiful things, the compendium of all interests and splendors.

No one paid attention to him; he did not share going to school in common with the other children, and he pried about everywhere. His forlornness obliged him to form his ideas spontaneously and to temper boldness with prudence.

While the children of his age were learning to read, he was walking around the wall, without being frightened by the crumbling stones, nor the brambles that closed the passage.

He knew where there were ringdoves, and he tried to gather up their nests; he stole fruit and picked wild blackberries and strawberries.

At the age of eight, Martin enjoyed a bad reputation, already worthy of a man. One day, on leaving school, Charles Ohando, the son of the rich family that left the house to Martin's mother out of charity, pointing to him with his finger, shouted:

"That guy! That guy is a thief."

"Me?" Martin exclaimed.

"Yes, you. The other day I saw you stealing pears at my house. Everybody in your family is a thief."

Martin, although in regard to him he could not deny the truth of the charge, thought that he should not permit this insult directed at the Zalacaíns, and, throwing himself at the young Ohando, he hit him hard with his fist. Ohando retaliated with a punch; they grabbed each other and fell to the ground; they tripped each other; but Martin, the stronger one, always beat his opponent. A sandal maker had to intervene in the fight, and by kicking and pushing, separated the two enemies. Martin went away triumphantly, and the young Ohando, bruised and beaten up, went off to his house.

Martin's mother, when she found out what had happened, tried to make her son go to the Ohando house and ask Charles to forgive him; but Martin affirmed that first they would have to kill him. She had to take the responsibility of giving the powerful family all kinds of excuses and explanations.

Since that time, the mother viewed her son as a reprobate.

"How did this boy get like that!" she would say; and she felt when she thought about him a confused feeling of love and grief, only comparable to the astonishment and despair of the hen when she hatches duck eggs and sees that her offspring are diving into the water without fear and are swimming about bravely.

Chapter II

Concerning the Old Cynic Michael Tellagorri

SOMETIMES, WHEN HIS MOTHER sent her son Martin to Arcale's tavern for wine or cider, she would say to him:

"And if you meet old Tellagorri, don't speak to him, and if he says something to you, just answer no to everything."

Tellagorri, Martin's great-uncle, the brother of his paternal grandmother, was a thin man with a huge hooked nose, gray hair, gray eyes, and a clay pipe always in his mouth. The principal figure in Arcale's tavern, he had his center of operations there: there he delivered speeches, debated, and kept alive the latent hatred that exists between the rustics and the landowner.

Old Tellagorri lived on a small amount of resources that he negotiated, and he had a bad reputation among the powerful people in town. He was, basically, a robber, happy and jovial, a good drinker, a good friend, and deep inside, rather violent, being capable of shooting someone or even setting the whole town on fire.

Martin's mother sensed that, given her son's character, he would end up by becoming a friend of Tellagorri, whom she considered a sinister man. As a matter of fact, that is the way it turned out; the same day on which the old man learned about the beating his nephew had given young Ohando, he took him under his protection and began to initiate him in his life.

The same noted day on which Martin gained Tellagorri's friendship, he also received the goodwill of Marquis. Marquis was Tellagorri's dog, a tiny, ugly dog, contaminated to such an extent with the ideas, concerns, and skills of his master, that he was just like him: an astute thief, a vagabond, old, cynical, unsociable, and independent. In addition, he shared Tellagorri's hatred for rich people, something unusual in a dog. If Marquis ever went into church, it was to see whether the children had left any breadcrumbs on the floor by the benches where they were sitting, not for any other reason. He had no mystical leanings. In spite of his aristocratic title, Marquis sympathized neither with the clergy nor with the nobility. Tellagorri always called him "Marquesch," an alteration which in Basque seems more affectionate.

Tellagorri owned a little orchard that was worthless according to the wise, at the end opposite his house, and to get to it, it was necessary to travel the entire balcony of the wall. Often people offered to buy the orchard from him, but he would say that it was a family possession and that the figs of his fig trees were so excellent that he would not sell that piece of ground for anything in the world.

Everyone believed that he kept the little orchard to have the right to go over the wall and steal, and this opinion was not, by any means, far from the truth.

Tellagorri belonged to the Galchagorri family, the family of the red trousers, and this rhyme, of the nickname and their surname, had served the father of the sexton's wife, a droll old man who hated Tellagorri, as a motive for a song that even the children knew and that deeply humiliated Tellagorri. The song went like this:

> *Tellagorri,*
> *Galchagorri,*
> *ongui etorri*
> *onerá.*
> *Ostutzale,*
> *erantzale,*
> *nescatzale,*
> *zu cerá.*

(Tellagorri, Galchagorri, welcome here are you. Fond of stealing, fond of drinking, fond of women, are you.)

Whenever Tellagorri heard the song, he would frown and become serious.

Tellagorri was a determined individualist; he had the individualism of the Basque reinforced and strengthened by the individualism of the Tellagorris.

"Everyone keeps what he has and steals what he can," he would say.

This was the most sociable of his theories; the more unsociable ones he kept to himself.

Tellagorri did not need anyone to get along. He made his own clothes; he shaved himself and cut his hair, made himself sandals, and he did not need anyone, neither woman nor man. At least that is the way he stated it.

When Tellagorri took Martin under his wing, he taught him everything he knew. He explained to him how to kill a hen with a blow on the neck without it making a noise; he showed him how to gather figs and plums from the orchards without danger of being seen, and he taught him to recognize good mushrooms from poisonous ones by the color of the grass in which they grew.

This harvesting of mushrooms and also hunting for snails constituted a source of income for Tellagorri, but the greatest source was something else.

There was in the Fortress, on one of the faces of the wall, a level place made of dirt which it seemed just as impossible to reach climbing up as going down. Nevertheless, Tellagorri found the path to get to that remote place, and in this hidden and sunny locale he put in an actual tobacco plantation, the dry leaves of which he would sell to the inn-keeper, Arcale.

The road that led to the old man's tobacco plantation went out from a piece of property owned by the Ohandos and passed over a foss of the Fortress. One could get to Tellagorri's remote place by opening an old and decayed gate found in this foss, and going up several moss-covered steps.

This road ascended on the thick roots of the trees, which constituted a stairway of uneven steps, enclosed in a tunnel of branches.

In the summer the leaves covered it completely. On hot August days one could sleep there in the shade, lulled by the chirping of the birds and the buzzing of the bumblebees.

The foss was also an interesting place for Martin; the walls were covered with red, yellow and green moss; between the stones the spurge, the henbane and the dwarf-elder grew, and the large, iridescent lizards tanned in the sun. In the gaps of the wall, barn owls and red owls would build their nests.

Tellagorri explained everything to Martin in detail.

Tellagorri was a wise man; no one knew the district as he did; no one mastered the geography of the Ibaya River, the plant and animal life of its banks and its waters as did this old cynic.

In the holes of the Roman bridge he kept his fishing tackle and his net for the closed season; he knew how to "hammer-fish," a process which consists of striking slabs of stone on the bottom of the river with a hammer and then raising them and gathering in the trout that were underneath and consequently remain stunned and motionless.

He could catch fish by shooting; he trapped otters in the cave of Amaviturrieta, which submerges in the ground and is half full of water; he cast his nets in Ocin beltz, the black hole where the river forms a pool; but he never used explosives, because, although only remotely, Tellagorri loved nature and did not want to impoverish it.

This old man also liked joking with people: he would say that nothing pleased otters as much as a newspaper with good news items, and he affirmed that if you left a paper on the banks of the river, these animals would come out to read it; he would tell extraordinary stories about the intelligence of salmon and other fish. In Tellagorri's mind, if dogs did not speak, it was because they did not want to, but he thought that they had as much intelligence as any human. This enthusiasm for dogs had caused him to make this disrespectful statement:

"I greet a poodle with more respect than I do the parish priest."

This pronouncement scandalized the town.

There were people who began to believe that Tellagorri and Voltaire had brought about modern impiety.

When the old man and the boy had nothing to do, they would go to the mountain to hunt with Marquis. Arcale would give Tellagorri his shotgun. Tellagorri, without any known motive, would begin to insult his dog. To do this he always had to use Spanish.

"Scoundrel! Bum!" he would say to him. "Filthy old dog! Coward!"

Marquis would answer the insults with a gentle bow-wow that seemed like a grumbling protest, would move his tail like a pendulum, and begin to roam about, sniffing all around. Suddenly he would detect movement in the weeds and lunge at them like an arrow.

Martin got a great deal of amusement from these spectacles. He was Tellagorri's companion for everything, except for going to the tavern: he did not want Martin there. At dusk, when he went to get involved in conversation with the group at Arcale's inn, he usually would say to him:

"All right, get off to my garden and pick some pears there, from the corner, and take them home. Tomorrow you'll give me the key."

And he would hand him a piece of iron that weighed at least half a ton.

Martin would walk along the balcony of the wall. Thus he knew that at So-and-so's house they had planted artichokes, and at What's-his-name's, beans. Seeing the gardens and the houses of others from atop the wall, and contemplating the labors of others, was gradually giving Martin a certain inclination toward a philosophy of life and theft.

Since basically young Zalacaín was a grateful lad and of good disposition, he felt for his old mentor great enthusiasm and great respect. Tellagorri knew it, although he pretended not to, but, in return for the boy's admiration and respect, he would do everything he knew that pleased the lad or that served for his education, if it was in his power.

And what remote places Tellagorri knew! As a good vagabond, he was fond of the contemplation of nature. The old man and the boy would go up to the heights of the Fortress, and there, stretched out on the grass and the furze, they would contemplate the extensive landscape. Spring afternoons were especially marvelous. The Ibaya River, clean and clear, traversed the valley amidst green farms and rows of very high poplars, widening and bounding over stones, then narrowing, changing into cascades of pearls on falling over the dike of the mill. Grim mountains closed the horizon, and in the orchards one could see small woods and groves of fruit trees.

The sun shone on the great elms with thick foliage of the Fortress, and reddened them and colored them with a copper tone.

Descending the heights, along goat paths, one would reach the clear waters of the Ibaya. Near the town, some reed fishermen usually spent the afternoon sitting on the banks, and the washwomen, with their bare legs in the river, would shake their clothes and sing.

Tellagorri recognized the fishermen from a distance: "There are So-and-so and What's-his-name," he would say. They surely have not caught anything. He would not join them; he knew of a remote place perfumed by the flowers of the acacia trees and the hawthorns where the river was in the shade and where the fish congregated.

Tellagorri hardened Martin; he made him walk, run, climb trees, get into holes like a ferret; he educated him in his own way, with the teaching method of the Tellagorris, which rather resembled savagery.

While other children were studying the gospel and the primer, Martin was contemplating the sights of nature; he would go into the cave of Erroitza, where there are immense rooms full of huge bats that hang from the walls by the claws of their membranous wings; he would bathe in Ocin beltz, in spite of the fact that the whole town considered this backwater extremely dangerous; he would hunt and take long trips.

Tellagorri had his grandson go into the river on one of the stagecoach horses when they took them in to bathe.

"Farther in! Closer to the dam, Martin!" he would say to him.

And Martin, laughing, would take the horses up to that very dam.

Some nights, Tellagorri took Zalacaín to the cemetery.

"Wait for me here a minute," he told him.

"Okay."

After a half hour, when he returned, he asked him:

"Were you afraid, Martin?"

"Afraid? Of what?"

"That's it! That's the way we've got to be," Tellagorri would say. "We've got to be firm, always firm."

Chapter III

The Gathering at Arcale's Inn

ARCALE'S INN WAS ON CASTLE STREET and formed a corner with Oquerra Lane. The lane went out to the gate of the old section. Arcale's house was a big house made of stone up to the second floor, and the rest was made of brick, which revealed its crossed beams blackened by moisture. It was both an inn and a tavern with the privileges of a club, since several residents of the "street" and some rustics gathered there at night to talk and debate, and on Sundays to get drunk. The vestibule, which was black, had a counter and a cabinet full of wines and cordials: on one side was the tavern, with long pine tables that could be raised and fastened to the wall, and in the back was the kitchen. Arcale was a heavy, active man, a former harvester and ex-horse dealer and smuggler. He had complicated accounts with everyone; he managed the stagecoaches, he was a clever dealer, a flatterer, and on holidays he added cooking to his many other occupations. He was always coming and going, talking, shouting, scolding his wife and his brother, the servants, and the poor: he was always busy doing something.

The evening gathering at Arcale's tavern was maintained by Tellagorri and Pichia. Pichia, a worthy comrade of Tellagorri, served as a contrast to him. Tellagorri dressed in dark colors; Pichia, perhaps to emphasize his bulk, dressed in light clothes; Tellagorri was considered poor; Pichia was rich; Tellagorri was liberal; Pichia, a Carlist; Tellagorri did not go to church; Pichia was always there; but, in spite of so many differences, Tellagorri and Pichia felt themselves spiritually aligned, fraternizing over a good glass of wine.

These two orators of Arcale's tavern, speaking Spanish, had a common characteristic, and it was that invariably they mixed-up their "f"s and "p"s. There was no way they could pronounce these letters correctly.

"What is your 'ofinion' of the new doctor?" Picha would ask Tellagorri.

"Pschaw!" the other would answer. "What he needs is 'fractice.'"

"Well, he's a clever man, a man of some 'portune'; he has a 'fiano' at home."

They both just could not pronounce these letters right.

Tellagorri was not very fond of things pertaining to the church; he had very little "pondness," as he would have said, and when he had two drinks too many, the first people about whom he would begin to speak badly were priests. It seemed natural that Pichia would get angry, and not only did he not get angry as a wax chandler and religious man, but he incited his friend so that he would say stronger things against the vicar, the assistants, the sacristan, or the sacristan's wife.

Nevertheless, Tellagorri respected the vicar of Arbea, whom the clergymen accused of being liberal and mad. This vicar had the custom of collecting his salary, changing it into silver, and leaving it on top of the table, forming a rather small pile, because the salary did not amount to much. Then, to each person who came to ask him for something, after rudely scolding him and reprimanding him for his vices and insulting him at times, he would give whatever seemed right, until by the middle of the month the heap of money was gone, and then he would give corn or beans, always grumbling and insulting.

Tellagorri would say: "That's a priest, not like those around here, who only want to live well and get good 'pees.'"

All Tellagorri's awkwardness in speaking Spanish turned into ease, rapidity, and elegance when he spoke in Basque. Nevertheless, he preferred speaking in Spanish because it seemed elegant to him.

Anything became amusing in the mouth of that old rascal.

When some pretty girl walked by the tavern, Tellagorri would let out such a sly, harsh sound that everyone would laugh.

Another man, doing the same thing, would have seemed common and uncouth; not he—Tellagorri had an inborn elegance and delicacy that removed him from rudeness.

He was also a man of proverbs, and when he was drunk he sang very badly, without any fondness whatsoever, but giving much malice to the words.

His two favorite songs were two hybrids of Basque and Spanish; translated literally, they did not mean a great deal, but on his lips they meant everything.

One, probably of his invention, went like this:

> *Ba dale sargentua,*
> *ba dale quefia,*
> *erreguiñen bizcarretic*
> *artzen ditu cafia.*
> *(Whether he be a sergeant or a commanding officer,*
> *he drinks his coffee at the queen's expense.)*

This, from Tellagorri's mouth, meant that everyone was a good-for-nothing.

The other song the old man kept for solemn moments, and it went like this:

> *Manuelacho, escasayozu*
> *barcasiyua Andresí.*
> *(Emmie, ask Andrew to forgive you.)*

And on saying this, Tellagorri bowed comically and continued with a twangy voice:

> *Beti orrela ibilli, gabe*
> *majo charraren iguesí.*
> *(Without always going about, in that way, fleeing from such a spruce little old man.)*

And then, as a serious consequence of what he had said before, he would add:

Part I: Zalacaín's Childhood

Napoleonen pauso gaiztoac
ondú dituzu icasi.
(You have learned well the bad ways of Napoleon.)

It was not easy to understand what bad ways of Napoleon Emmie might have learned. Emmie probably did not even have the remotest idea of the existence of the hero of Austerlitz, but this did not prevent the song in the mouth of Tellagorri from being extremely amusing.

For the times when Tellagorri was somewhat aroused or drunk, he had a bilingual song, in which the embrace of Vergara was celebrated, and which concluded like this:

¡Viva Espartero! ¡Viva erreguiña!
¡Ojalá de repente ilcobalizaque
bere ama ciquiña!
(Long live Expartero! Long live the queen! Oh how I wish that her dirty
mother would suddenly die!)

This adjective, addressed to the mother of Isabella II, indicated to what extent the hatred for María Cristina had reached even the most distant corners of Spain.

Chapter IV

Referring to the Noble House of Ohando

AT THE ENTRANCE TO the new town, on the road and, therefore, outside the walls, was the oldest and most noble house in Urbia: the house of Ohando.

For a long time the Ohando family formed the town's only aristocracy: in the distant past they were great landholders and founders of chaplaincies; then some reverses of fortune and the civil war depleted their income, and the arrival of other rich families took from them the absolute supremacy they had had.

The Ohando house was on the road, but far enough away from it to leave room for a beautiful garden, in which, as if standing guard, stood six magnificent linden trees. Between the huge trunks of these trees grew old rosebushes, which formed garlands in the spring, loaded with flowers.

Another climbing rosebush, with twisted branches and tea-colored roses, ascended the facade, spreading like a grapevine, and it gave a delicate and airy tone to the big old house. This garden also had, on the side that joined with the fruit garden, a grove of lilac and elder trees. In the months of April and May these plants bloomed and mingled their perfumed thyrsuses, their white corollas, and their blue clusters.

On the ancestral house, over the huge central balcony, the coat of arms of the founders, carved in red sandstone, was prominently displayed; on it there were engraved two rampant wolves with disjoined hands in their mouths and an oak tree in the background. In heraldic language, the wolf indicates cruelty with enemies, the oak tree, venerable old age.

Judging by the heraldry of the Ohandos, they were from an old family, ferocious with their enemies. If credence could be given to some old stories, the coat of arms told nothing but the truth.

The back part of the house of the noblemen faced a ravine; it had a huge glass gallery and was made of brick, with a black framework; in front rose a two-thousand-foot mount, according to the map of the province, with some rows of houses on the lower part, and devoid of vegetation and only covered at intervals by evergreen and pin oaks on the upper part.

On one side, the garden was prolonged by a magnificent sloping fruit garden, facing south.

The Ohando family consisted of the mother, Agueda, and her children, Charles and Catherine.

Agueda, a weak, fanatic, and sickly woman, of very little character, was consistently dominated in household matters by some old servant woman, and in spiritual matters by her confessor.

At this time the confessor was a young priest named Felix, a man of calm and sweet appearance who concealed obscure ambitions for power under a cloak of evangelical meekness.

Charles Ohando, Agueda's oldest child, was a rough, gloomy, shy boy, with violent passions. Hatred and envy became veritable illnesses in him.

He had hated Martin Zalacaín since his early childhood; when Martin beat him up, as he came out of school, Charles' hatred became rage. When he saw Martin riding his horse and going into the river, he would wish for a perilous stumble.

He hated him madly.

Catherine, instead of being gloomy and rough like her brother Charles, was lively, cheerful, gay, and very pretty. When she went to school, with her rosy little face, her gray dress, and a red beret on her blonde head, all the women of the town would caress her; the other girls always wanted to walk with her, and they said that, in spite of her privileged position, she was not at all proud.

One of her friends was little Ignacia, Martin's sister.

Catherine and Martin met each other often and talked; he would see her from the top of the wall, in the belvedere of the house, cutely seated and very proper, playing or learning to do hose. She was always hearing about Martin's escapades.

"That devil's up there on the wall," Agueda would say. "He's going to kill himself one of these days. What a devil of a boy! How bad he is!"

Catherine knew by this time that the words "that devil" referred to Martin.

Charles had once said to his sister:

"Don't speak to that thief."

But Catherine did not think it was any crime for Martin to pick fruit from the trees and to eat it, nor to run along the wall. She fancied foolish things, because since she had been a little girl she had had an instinct for order and tranquility, and it seemed bad to her that Martin was so crazy.

The Ohandos were owners of a garden next to the river with huge magnolias and linden trees, and surrounded by a bramble fence.

When Catherine would go there with the maidservant to pick flowers, Martin often followed them and remained at the entrance of the fence.

"Come in if you like," Catherine would say to him.

"Okay," and Martin would go in and speak about his excursions, about the wild things he was going to do, and he would expound Tellagorri's opinions, which to him seemed to be articles of faith.

"It would be better for you to go to school!" Catherine told him.

"Me go to school?" Martin exclaimed. "I'll go to America or to the war."

Catherine and the servant would enter by a path of the garden full of rosebushes and they would make bouquets of flowers. Martin would see them and contemplate the dam, the waters of which glistened in the sun like pearls and burst into very white foam.

"I would go over there if I had a boat," Martin would say.

Catherine would protest:

"Are you always going to think only about foolish things? Why aren't you like the other children?"

"I can beat all of them," Martin would answer, as if this were a reason.

In the spring, the road next to the river was delightful. The new leaves of the beech trees began to turn green; the fern cast its twisted sprouts to the air; the apple and pear trees of the gardens displayed their snow-white flowered branches, and one could hear the singing of the redwings and the nightingales in the bowers. The sky appeared blue, a soft blue, somewhat pale, and only a white cloud or two, with crude outlines, as if made of marble, could be seen.

On Saturday afternoons, during the spring and the summer, Catherine and other girls from the town, accompanied by some good woman, would go to the cemetery. Each one carried a little basket of flowers, made a whiskbroom out of dry weeds, cleaned the ground by the gravestones where their deceased relatives were buried, and adorned the crosses with roses and white lilies. On their way back home together, they would see how the stars were beginning to shine in the sky, and they would listen to the toads, which let out their mysterious flute notes in the silence of the dusk…

Often, in the month of May, when Tellagorri and Martin passed by the riverbank, as they crossed behind the church, they could hear the voices of the girls, who were singing in chorus the praises of the Virgin.

Emenchen gauzcatzu, ama.
(Here we are, mother.)

They would listen for a moment, and Martin could make out the voice of Catherine, the Ohando girl.

"It's Catherine, the Ohando girl," Martin would say.

"If you aren't a fool, you'll marry her," Tellagorri would reply.

And Martin would start laughing.

Chapter V

How Martin Lopez Zalacaín
Died in the Year of Our Lord 1412

ONE OF THE CITIZENS who most frequently walked along the path of the wall was an old gentleman named Fermin Soraberri. For many, many years Fermin held the office of secretary of the municipal government of Urbia until he retired when his daughter married a rather prosperous farmer.

Mr. Fermin Soraberri was a tall, big, heavy man with swollen eyelids and a puffed face. He usually wore a small cap with two ribbons hanging in the back, a blue cape and low shoes. Fermin's specialty was absent-mindedness. He forgot everything. His narratives were cut short by this dominant characteristic:

> 'Once, in Oñate...' (For Mr. Soraberri, Oñate was the modern Athens. In Spain there are twenty or thirty modern Athenses.) 'Once, in Oñate, I succeeded in witnessing something extremely interesting. I, the vicar and an elementary school teacher were gathered together, and...' and Mr. Soraberri looked all around, as if frightened, with his big, turbid eyes and said: "Where was I? Well, ... I've forgotten the matter.'

Mr. Soraberri always forgot the matter. Almost every day the ex-secretary met Tellagorri and they exchanged a greeting and some words about the weather and the progress of the fruit trees. When he began to see him accompanied by Martin, Mr. Soraberri was surprised and looked at the boy with his air of a swollen and softened elephant.

He thought about asking him some questions but he put it off for several days because Mr. Soraberri was slow at everything. Finally he said to him, with his majestic slowness:

"Whose boy is this, Tellagorri old friend?"

"This boy? He's a relative of mine."

"One of the Tellagorris?"

"No, his name is Martin Zalacaín."

"Oh, man! Oh, man! Martin Lopez Zalacaín."

"No, not Lopez," said Tellagorri.

"I know what I'm talking about. This boy's real name is Martin Lopez Zalacaín and he must be from that settlement near the gate of France."

"Yes, sir; that's where he's from."

"Well, I am familiar with his history, and he has been Lopez Zalacaín and he will be Lopez Zalacaín, and if you like, come to my house tomorrow and I'll read a paper to you that I copied in the archives of City Hall concerning this matter."

Tellagorri said he would come and in fact, the next day, thinking that what the ex-secretary had said might be of some importance, he arrived at his house with Martin.

Mr. Soraberri had forgotten the matter but he soon remembered what it was about; he instructed his daughter to bring Tellagorri a glass of wine, went into his study and returned shortly afterward with some old papers in his hand; he put on his glasses, cleared his throat, shifted his notes, and said:

"Oh! Here it is. This," he added, "is a copy of a narrative done by the chronicler Iñigo Sanchez Ezpeleta concerning how the first blood was shed in the war of the lineages, in Urbia, between the house of Ohando and the house of Zalacaín, and he assumed that these fights began in our town at the end of the fourteenth or beginning of the fifteenth century."

"And was that a long time ago?" Tellagorri asked.

"Almost five hundred years."

"And did the Zalacaíns already exist then?"

"Not only did they exist, but they were nobles."

"Listen, listen," said Tellagorri, hitting Martin, who was becoming distracted, with his elbow.

"Do you want me to read what the chronicler says?"

"Yes, yes."

"Fine. Well, it goes like this: 'Title: How Martin Lopez Zalacaín Died in the Year of Our Lord 1412.'"

After he had read this, he coughed, spit, and began this account with great solemnity:

"There was a noted ancient enmity between the house of Ohando, which is in the kingdom of Navarre, and the house of Zalacaín, which is in the Borte land. And it is said that the cause of the enmity was envy and the attempt to prove which was the better, and they performed much witchcraft and the Zalacaíns burned Mr. St. Peter alive in a fight which they waged on the plain of Somo, and because this Mr. St. Peter left no son, they married his daughter to Martin Lopez Zalacaín, a very restless man.

"And this Martin Lopez, having come to the town of Urbia, was challenged by Mosen St. Peter, of the house of Ohando, who was a nephew of the other Mr. St. Peter and who had cast many spells and done much ambushing and stealing.

"And Martin Lopez answered his challenge: As you know, I am considered here the most valiant and skillful man with weapons in all this land, and it seems that the Ohandos have brought you, because you are the best lancer in Navarre, to avenge the death of my father-in-law, who fought in the loyally waged battle at Somo, and just as he wanted to kill me, so did I want to kill him.

"And so if it would please you for us to meet in single combat, until one of us or both of us by chance should die, I would be most happy to oblige and soon.

"And Mosen St. Peter replied that he was satisfied, and they agreed to meet on the meadow of Saint Ann. At the appointed time this Martin Lopez arrived on his horse like a valiant knight, and before he had a chance to fight Mosen St. Peter he was wounded by an arrow that penetrated his eye, and he fell dead from his horse in the middle of the meadow. And they hamstrung him. And the man who planned the ambush and shot the crossbow was Velche Micolalde, a relative and friend of Mosen St. Peter Ohando. And Martin Lopez's men, when they saw him dead and since there were but few of them facing the Ohando men, were very much afraid and they all began to flee.

"And when Martin Lopez's wife found out about it, she went to the meadow of Saint Ann, and when she saw her husband's bloody, wounded body, she knelt down, took him in her arms and began to cry, cursing the war and her misfortune. And this happened in the year of Our Lord, 1412."

When he finished, Mr. Soraberri looked, through his spectacles, at his two listeners. Martin had not learned anything; Tellagorri said:

"Yes, those Ohandos are 'two-pased.' They go to church a lot, and then they kill like devils."

Soraberri effectively suggested to his friend Tellagorri that he never make venturesome, rash judgments, and with this idea he began to tell a story which had actually taken place in Oñate; but as he was about to specify the individuals who had taken part in his story, he forgot the matter and he regretted it, he truly regretted it, because, as he said, he was sure that the deed was extremely interesting and, besides, very worthy of mention.

Chapter VI

About the Arrival of Some Traveling Showmen and What Happened Afterward

ONE DAY IN MAY, at dusk, three wagons pulled by thin horses full of sores and spavins appeared on the main road. They passed through the new section of the town and stopped at the high part of the meadow of Saint Ann.

Tellagorri, the information center of Arcale's tavern, had to know right away what was happening, so he showed up at once on the spot, followed by Marquis.

He immediately began a conversation with the leader of the caravan, and after several questions and answers and the man telling him he was French and a tamer of wild animals, Tellagorri took him to Arcale's tavern.

Martin also found out about the arrival of the trainers with their caged beasts, and the next morning, when he got up, the first thing he did was go to the meadow of Saint Ann.

The sun was beginning to come out when the tamer's camp arrived.

One of the wagons was the home of the quacks. The tamer, his wife, an old man, a boy, and a girl had just come out. Only a baby girl a few months old remained in the wagon-hut playing with a dog.

The tamer did not have that half-flippant, half-grotesque air so common to traveling actors and fair people: he was somber, young, with a gypsy quality, black, curly hair, green eyes, a mustache lengthened at the ends by small side-whiskers, and an expression of sinister, repulsive wickedness.

The old man, the woman, and the children looked like typical poor people; they belonged to those types and blurred figures that the die of poverty produces by the thousands.

The man, aided by the old man and the boy, traced a circle in the ground with a rope, and in the center he placed a big pole, from the end of which several ropes extended, that were tied to stakes driven firmly in the ground.

The tamer looked for Tellagorri to borrow a ladder from him; Tellagorri explained that there was one at Arcale's tavern; they got it from there and used it to fasten the canvases until they formed a conical-shaped tent.

They placed the two wagons with cages in which they kept the wild animals so as to leave a space between them, which served as an entrance to the circus, and on top and on the sides the quacks put up three daubed posters. One showed several dogs lunging at a bear; the other, a fight between a lion and a buffalo, and the third, some Indians with lances attacking a tiger that was waiting for them on the branch of a tree as if it were a linnet.

The men put the finishing touches on the circus, and on Sunday, just as the people were coming out from vespers, the tamer appeared, followed by the old man, in the square of Urbia, in front of the church. Facing the assembled townspeople the tamer began to blow a hunting horn, and his assistant gave a drum roll.

The two men traversed the streets of the old district and then went out beyond the gates, and going along the bridge, followed by a mob of boys and girls, they arrived at the meadow of Saint Ann, approached the camp quarters and stopped there.

At the entrance the woman was playing the bass drum with her right hand and the cymbals with her left, and a girl with disheveled hair was shaking a little bell. To these discordant sounds were joined the sharp notes of the hunting horn and the drum roll, altogether producing an unbearable noise.

This noise ceased at an imperious signal from the tamer, who, with his wind instrument on his left arm, approached a stepladder next to the entrance, went up two or three rungs, took a rod, and, pointing to the hideous figures daubed on the canvases, said in an emphatic voice:

"Here you will see the bears, the wolves, the lion, and other terrible beasts. You will see the fight of the bear from the Pyrenees with the dogs, which jump on him and end up by overcoming him. This is the lion of the wilderness, whose roars scare the bravest of hunters. His voice alone frightens the most valiant heart... listen!"

The tamer paused a moment, and from inside the hut one could hear terrible roars, and, as if answering them, the ferocious barking of a dozen dogs.

The audience was terrified.

"In the wilderness..."

The tamer was going to continue, but seeing that the effect of curiosity on the audience was achieved, and that the crowd was trying to get inside the circus without delay, he shouted:

"The entrance charge is only one *real*. Step forward, ladies and gentlemen! Step forward!"

And again he struck a martial note with the hunting horn while the old assistant rolled the drum.

The woman opened the canvas that closed the door and began to collect the coins from those who were entering.

Martin witnessed all these procedures with a growing curiosity; he would have given anything to get in but he had no money.

He looked for an opening between the canvases so that he could see something, but he could not find one; he stretched out on the ground, and he was in that position, with his face near the ground, when the tamer's ragged girl, who was ringing the little bell at the door, came up to him.

"Hey, you, what are you doing there?"

"Looking," said Martin.

"You can't."

"And why can't I?"

"Because you can't. If you don't believe me, stay there. You'll see if my master catches you."

"And who is your master?"

"Who do you think? The tamer."

"Oh! But, you're from here?"

"Yes."

"And you don't know how to get in?"

"If you don't say anything to anyone, I'll get you in."

"Then I'll bring you cherries."

"From where?"

"I know where there are some.

"What's your name?"

"Martin. And yours?"

"Mine's Linda."

"That was the name of the doctor's dog," Martin said, not very gallantly.

Linda did not object to the comparison; she went behind the entrance to the circus, pulled on a canvas, opened a crack, and said to Martin:

"Come on, go in."

Martin slipped through, followed by the girl.

"When will you give me the cherries?" she asked.

"When this is over, I'll go get them."

Martin went into the audience. The show that the wild animal tamer presented was really repulsive. Around the circus, tied to the legs of a bench made of boards, were ten or twelve thin, mangy dogs. The tamer cracked his whip and all the dogs together began to bark and howl furiously. Then the man came with a bear tied to a chain, its head protected by a leather covering.

The tamer made the bear stand up several times and dance with the pole crossed over its shoulders and play the tambourine. Then he let a dog loose and the dog rushed at the bear, and, after a brief struggle, it caught hold of the bear's hide. Then the tamer let another dog loose, and another and another, with which the audience began to tire.

Martin did not think this was fair because the poor bear was defenseless. The dogs leaped so furiously at the bear that in order to get them to let go of their prey the tamer or the old man had to bite their tails. The show displeased Martin and he said so out loud, and some of the other people agreed with him, about the fact that the bear, being tied up, was unable to defend itself.

But then they tormented the poor beast even more. The tamer was a real scoundrel and he hit the animal on the paws, and the bear driveled and let out a few stifled groans.

"That's enough! That's enough!" shouted a prosperous traveler who had been in California.

"You're only doing that because you have the bear tied up," Martin said. "If you didn't, you wouldn't try anything like that."

With a look of hatred in his eyes, the tamer stared at the boy.

What followed was more pleasant: the tamer's wife, wearing a spangled dress, went into the lion's cage, played with it, made it jump and stand up, and then Linda performed a few acrobatic feats and came out with a little monkey dressed in red, which she had do some acrobatic tricks.

The show came to an end. The people were getting ready to leave. Martin noticed that the tamer was looking at him. Without a doubt he had been paying close attention to him. Martin moved forward toward the exit and the tamer said to him:

"Wait, you haven't paid. Now we'll have it out. I'm going to let the dogs get you the way they got the bear."

Martin stepped back frightened; the tamer was looking at him with a vicious smile on his face. Martin remembered the place where he had gotten in, and impetuously pushing the canvas, he opened it and made his exit from the hut. The tamer was sorry to see him get away. Then Martin went around the meadow of Saint Ann, until he wisely stopped some fifteen or twenty yards from the circus entrance.

When he saw Linda he said:

"Do you want to come?"

"I can't."

"Well, I'll bring you the cherries now."

Just as he was speaking he saw the tamer running toward him; he doubtless intended to take Martin; but, realizing that he would not catch him, he took his vengeance on the girl and gave her a brutal slap. The little girl fell to the ground. Some women got between them and prevented the tamer from striking poor Linda any more.

"You let him in, didn't you?" the tamer shouted in French.

"No, he got in by himself."

"You're lying. It was you. Confess or I'll break your neck."

"Yes, I did it."

"And why?"

"Because he told me he would bring me cherries."

"Oh! Okay," and the tamer calmed down, "let him bring them; but if you eat them, I'll beat you to death. And you know I will."

A little later Martin returned with his cap full of cherries. Linda put them in her apron, and had them there when the tamer appeared again. Martin jumped backwards.

"No, don't run away," said the tamer, trying to put on a friendly smile.

Martin stayed. Then the man asked him who he was, and when he discovered his relationship to Tellagorri, he said to him:

"Come whenever you like; I'll let you in."

For the rest of the week the tamer's hut was empty. On Sunday the quacks had the town crier make an announcement, saying that they would perform an extraordinary and interesting act. Martin told his mother and sister. The girl became frightened when she heard the story about the wild animals, and she refused to go.

Only Martin and his mother came. The extraordinary act was the fight between Linda and the bear. The little girl appeared nude from the waist up wearing red percale slacks, hugged the bear, and acted as if she were fighting it, but the tamer was frequently pulling on a rope tied to the bear's nose.

In spite of the fact that the people thought that there was no danger to the girl, seeing the huge, shaggy claws of the animal on the girl's feeble shoulders produced a horrifying impression.

After the extraordinary act, which did not enthuse the audience, the woman went into the lion's cage.

The animal must have been sick because the woman tamer, despite all her efforts, could not get it to do the usual tricks.

Seeing this calamity the tamer, overcome by a mad rage, entered the cage, ordered the woman to get out, and started lashing the lion with a whip. The lion got up showing its teeth, and with a mighty roar leaped at the tamer; the old assistant put an iron rod between the cage bars to separate the man from the animal, but as luck would have it, the rod got caught on the tamer's clothes, and instead of protecting him, it immobilized him and left him at the lion's mercy.

The audience saw the tamer bleeding and they got to their feet terrified and ready to run away.

There was no danger to the spectators, but people began to panic and rush in confusion toward the exit; someone, no one ever found out who, fired a shot at the lion, and in that mad moment of escape several women and children were mangled and bruised.

The tamer was also seriously injured.

Two women were picked up badly bruised; one of them was an old woman from a distant village who had not been in Urbia for ten years; the other was Martin's mother, who, besides the bruises and blows, had a wound on her neck, caused, according to what the doctor said, by a piece of the cage bar, which had come loose when the bullet fired by an unknown person struck it.

They took Martin's mother to her house, and whether the bruises and wound were that serious, or whether, as some said, she was not well cared for, the fact was that the poor woman died a week after the accident in the hut, leaving Martin and Ignacia orphans.

Chapter VII

How Tellagorri Could
Protect His Own

WHEN MARTIN'S MOTHER DIED, Tellagorri, to the town's great astonishment, got his nephew and niece and took them to his house. Mrs. Ohando said that it was a pity that those children had to live with an impious man, without religion and conventional manners, capable of saying that he greeted a poodle with more respect than the parish priest.

The good lady lamented, but she did nothing, and Tellagorri took the responsibility of caring for and feeding the orphans.

Ignacia went to Arcale's inn, and worked there as a servant girl until she was fourteen.

Martin attended school for a few months, but Tellagorri had to take him out before the end of the school year because he got into fights with all the boys and he even tried to whip the teacher.

Arcale, who knew that the boy was clever and had a lively disposition, used him as a messenger on the coach to France; and when he learned to drive, they promoted him from messenger to temporary coachman and, at the end of a year, made him a regular driver.

Martin, at the age of sixteen, was earning his own living and was at the height of his glory. He boasted of being a little fierce and he dressed somewhat flamboyantly, with the spruce elegance of the old postilions. He wore colored vests and on his watch chain he had silver charms. On Sundays he liked to show off in town; but no less did he like on workdays to ride in the coachbox along the highway cracking the whip, to go in the inns along the road, to tell and hear stories and to run errands.

Mrs. Ohando and Catherine had him do errands frequently, and they advised him to bring them fabrics, lace, and sometimes jewels from France.

"How is it going, Martin?" Catherine would say to him in Basque.

"Okay," he answered rudely, making himself more the man. "And you and your family?"

"Everyone's fine. When you go to France you have to buy me some lace like the other time. You know?"

"Yeah, sure; I'll buy you some."

"Do you know French already?"

"I'm just starting to speak it."

Martin was becoming a big man, tall, strong, resolute. He abused his strength and bravery somewhat, but he never attacked the weak. He also distinguished himself as a *pelota* player and was one of the best racket players.

One winter Martin did something that caused a lot of talk in the town. The road was impassable because of the snow and the coach could not get through. Zalacaín went to France and came back on foot, by way of Navarre, with a resident of Larraun. The two of them traveled through the Irati forest and several wild boars attacked them.

Neither man was armed, but using sticks they killed three of those wild animals—Zalacaín killed two and the man from Larraun the other.

When Martin returned home triumphantly, suffering from fatigue and with his two wild boars, the whole town considered him a hero.

Tellagorri also received many compliments for having such a brave, bold nephew. The old man, very happy, although pretending to be indifferent, said:

"This nephew of mine is going to cause a lot of talk. It runs in the family. Because I don't know if you've ever heard anything about Lopez Zalacaín. No? Well, ask that old Soraberri and you'll find out..."

"And what does that Lopez have to do with your nephew?" they would reply.

"Well, he's Martin's ancestor. You don't understand anything."

Tellagorri paid dearly for the triumph his nephew had achieved in the wild boar hunt, because he got sick from drinking so much.

Ignacia and Martin, on the doctor's advice, made the old man cut off all drinks, whether wine or liquor; but Tellagorri, because he had to abstain, languished and became more and more sad.

"Without wine and without whiskey I'm a dead man," Tellagorri would say. And seeing that the truth of this statement did not convince the doctor, he had them call another, younger one.

This one let the drunkard have his way, and not only did he advise him to drink a little whiskey every day but he prescribed some medicine made with rum. Ignacia had to hide the bottle of medicine so that the patient would not drink it all in one gulp. As the alcohol entered Tellagorri's body, the old man was straightening up and growing lively.

After a week's treatment he felt so well that he began to get up and go to Arcale's inn; but he thought he could do some foolish things, in spite of his age, and he went out at night in the snow and caught pleurisy.

"You won't recover this time," the doctor told him, upset when he saw that his prescriptions had not been effective.

Tellagorri understood, became serious, made a quick confession, put his things in order, and, calling Martin to his side, said to him in Basque:

"Martin, my son, I am going away. Don't cry. It doesn't matter to me. You're strong and brave and a good boy. Don't leave your sister; look after her. For the time being, the best thing you can do is take her to the Ohandos. She flirts a little but Catherine will take her. Don't forget Marquesch either; he's old but he has done his part."

"No, I won't forget him," said Martin, sobbing.

"Now," Tellagorri continued, "I am going to tell you something, and it is that before very long there will be a war. You're brave, Martin; you won't be afraid of the bullets. Go to the war, but don't go as a soldier. Neither with the whites nor with the blacks. To business, Martin! To business! You'll sell to the liberals and to the Carlists; you'll make your venture and you'll marry the Ohando girl. If you have a son, name him after me: Michael or Joseph Michael."

"Sure," said Martin, without paying attention to the extravagant nature of the advice.

"Tell Arcale," the old man continued saying, "where I have the tobacco and the mushrooms. Now come closer. When I die, search my bed and you'll find at this end on the left a sock with some gold coins in it. As I've already told you, I don't want you to spend them on land, but on business goods."

"I will."

"I think I've told you everything. Now give me your hand. Firm, right?"

"Firm."

Poor Tellagorri forgot to say *"pirm,"* as he would have had he been well.

"That dull Ignacia," the old man continued after a brief pause, "you can give her whatever you think when she gets married."

Martin said yes to everything. Then he kept the old man company, answering his questions, some of which were very strange, and at dawn Michael Tellagorri, a man with a bad reputation and a good heart, died.

Chapter VIII

How the Hatred Between Martin Zalacaín and Charles Ohando Increased

WHEN TELLAGORRI DIED, CATHERINE Ohando, already a young lady, spoke to her mother about bringing Ignacia, Martin's sister, to their house. Ignacia was, as the talk got around, somewhat flirtatious, and she was accustomed to the flattery of the people at Arcale's place.

The belief that the girl, if she continued to work at the tavern, might develop a bad reputation, influenced Mrs. Ohando to bring her to her house as a maid. She intended to lecture her until she had removed all her bad habits, and she would attempt to direct her along the path of the strictest virtue.

With the purpose of seeing his sister, Martin went several times to the Ohando house and spoke with Catherine and Agueda. Catherine continued to speak familiarly to him, and Agueda showed affection and sympathy for him, which she expressed in an endless number of warnings and bits of advice.

Charles Ohando, on vacation from the Colegio de Oñate, arrived home in the summertime.

Martin soon noticed that, with the absence, the hatred that Charles had for him had increased rather than diminished. When he confirmed that this was indeed the case, he stopped coming to the Ohando house.

"You don't come to see us anymore," Catherine said to him once when she met him on the street.

"I don't come because your brother hates me," answered Martin, clearly.

"No, don't be silly."

"Bah! I know what I'm talking about."

The hatred did exist. It was shown first of all in the pelota game.

Martin had a rival in a boy from Navarre, from the Ribera del Ebro, the son of a carabineer.

They called this rival Lefty because he was left-handed.

Charles Ohando and some of his fellow students, who were Carlists pretending to be aristocrats, began to protect Lefty, to arouse him, and to make him challenge Martin.

Lefty played the furious game of a small, passionate man; Martin's game, calm and quiet, was that of one who is sure of himself. Lefty, if he began to win, got excited and carried out the match expeditiously; on the other hand if he got discouraged he made nothing but mistakes.

They were two types, Zalacaín and Lefty, completely distinct: the one had the serenity and intelligence of the mountain dweller, the other, the fury and strength of the people from the river country.

Such a rivalry, exploited by Ohando and his group of young men, ended in a match that Lefty's friends proposed. They agreed to the following contest: Lefty and Isquiña, an old player from Urbia, against Zalacaín and whatever partner he might choose. The match would be with rackets and consist of ten games.

Martin chose as his backstop a French-Basque lad who worked at the Archipi bakery and whose name was Bautista Urbide.

Bautista was thin but strong, cool and very much in control of himself.

A lot of money was bet on both sides. Almost all the popular and liberal group were for Zalacaín and Urbide; the young gentlemen, the sacristan and the Carlist people from the settlements, for Lefty.

The match was a big event in Urbia; the whole town and many people from the surrounding areas went to the pelota game to witness the spectacle.

The main contest was going to be between the two forwards, Zalacaín and Lefty. Lefty had on his side his nervousness, his fury, his force in throwing the ball low and in the corner; Zalacaín trusted in his serenity, his good vision and the strength of his arm, which allowed him to catch the ball and hurl it a long way.

The mountains against the plains.

The match began amidst a great expectation; the first few games were brought to full speed by Lefty, who tossed the balls like bullets just fractions of an inch above the stripe, so that it was impossible to pick them up.

At every masterly stroke of the Navarrese, the young gentlemen and the Carlists applauded enthusiastically; Zalacaín smiled and Bautista looked at him with a certain reserved panic.

The score was four to nothing and the victory of the Navarrese seemed a sure thing when the luck changed and Zalacaín and his partner began to win.

At first Lefty defended himself well and ended the game with furious blows; but then, as if he had lost energy, he started making errors one after another, and the match was tied.

From then on it was obvious that Lefty and Isquiña were losing the contest. They were demoralized. Lefty lunged angrily at the ball; he committed an error and became enraged; he hit his racket furiously on the ground and blamed his backstop for everything.

Zalacaín and the French-Basque, masters of the situation, kept completely cool, ran elastically and laughed.

"There, Bautista," Zalacaín would say. "Good!"

"Run, Martin," shouted Bautista. "That's the way!"

The contest ended with the total triumph of Zalacaín and Urbide.

"*Viva guatarrac!*" ("Long live our people") shouted those from the "street" of Urbia, applauding rudely.

Catherine smiled at Martin and congratulated him several times.

"Very good! Very good!"

"We did what we could," he answered, smiling.

Charles Ohando went up to Martin and said to him with deep frown:

"Lefty will play you in singles."

"I'm tired," Zalacaín responded.

"Don't you want to play?"

"No. You play if you want to."

Charles, who had once more verified his sister's sympathy for Martin, felt his hatred becoming inflamed.

Charles Ohando had come from Oñate that time more gloomy, more fanatic, and more violent than ever.

Martin was aware of the hatred of Catherine's brother, and when he met him by chance he would quickly get away, which only made Charles more angry and furious.

Martin was worried looking for a way to follow Tellagorri's advice and to devote himself to business. He had left his job as coachman and gone into the smuggling trade with Arcale.

One day an old servant woman from the Ohando house, a gossip and backbiter, went to look for him and told him that Ignacia, his sister, was flirting with Charles, the young Ohando.

If Agueda noticed it she would dismiss Ignacia, with which the scandal would leave the girl in a bad situation.

Martin, when he found out, felt like going to Charles and insulting him and challenging him. Later, considering that the main thing was to avoid gossip, he planned several things, until, finally, it seemed to him best to go see his friend Bautista Urbide. He had seen the French-Basque dancing with Ignacia many times, and thought he had some affection for her.

The same day he learned the news he appeared at Archipi's bakery, where Urbide was working. He found the French-Basque, naked from the waist up, at the mouth of the oven.

"Listen, Bautista," he said.

"What is it?"

"I have to talk to you."

"I'm listening," the Frenchman stated, while manipulating the baker's peel.

"Do you like Nasi, my sister?"

"Man… yeah! What a question!" exclaimed Bautista. "And for that you came to see me?"

"Would you marry her?"

"If I had money to settle down, sure I would."

"How much would you need?"

"About eighty or a hundred *duros*."

"I'll give it to you."

"And why the hurry? Is anything wrong with Ignacia?"

"No, but I've found out that Charles Ohando is making love to her. And since he has her in his house!"

"Say no more, say no more. Speak to her, and if she wants to, it's done. We'll get married right away."

Bautista and Martin said goodbye, and the next day Martin called his sister and reproached her for her flirtation and stupidity. Ignacia denied the rumors her brother had heard; but finally, she confessed that Charles was courting her, but with a good purpose.

"With a good purpose!" exclaimed Zalacaín. "Oh, you are dumb, child."

"Why?"

"Because he only wants to deceive you."

"He told me he'd marry me."

"And you believed him?"

"Me! I told him to wait and that I'd ask you, but he answered that he doesn't want me to tell you anything."

"Of course. Because I'd ruin his plans. He wants to deceive you and dishonor us, and he wants the whole town to scorn us because he hates me. I only have one thing to say to you: if anything happens between you and that guy, I'll skin the both of you, and I'll set the house on fire, at the risk of being put in prison for life."

Ignacia began to cry, but when Martin told her that Bautista wanted to marry her and that he had money, she quickly dried her tears.

"Bautista wants to get married?" Ignacia asked, surprised.

"Yes."

"But, he doesn't have any money!"

"Well, he has found some."

The idea of marrying Bautista not only consoled the girl but also seemed to offer her a promising future.

"And what do you want me to do? Leave the house?" Ignacia asked, drying her tears and smiling.

"No, for the time being, stay there; that's the best thing to do, and in a few days Bautista will go see Agueda and tell her he's marrying you."

The agreement between the two was carried out. In the days that followed, Charles Ohando saw that his conquest was not progressing, and on Sunday, in the square, he conclusively verified that Ignacia was definitely interested in Bautista. The girl and the baker danced very enthusiastically all afternoon.

Charles waited for Ignacia to be alone, then he insulted her and told her to her face that she was a flirt and a fake. The girl, who really had no great interest in Charles, when she saw how violent he was acting, became cold and fearful.

Shortly afterward, Bautista Urbide went to the Ohando house, spoke to Agueda, the wedding took place, and Bautista and Ignacia went to live in Zaro, a small town in the French-Basque territory.

Chapter IX

How Charles Tried to Take Revenge on Martin Zalacaín

CHARLES OHANDO BECAME ILL with rage. His nature, violent and proud, could not bear the humiliation of being beaten; just the thought of it mortified him and corroded his soul.

When Charles tried to seduce Ignacia, his hatred for Martin influenced him almost more than his affection for the girl. He was fascinated with the idea of dishonoring her and making Martin's life sad. Basically, Zalacaín's self-possession, his contentment with living, his ease in behaving overconfidently, offended this gloomy, fanatic man.

Besides, in Charles, the idea of order, of rank, of subordination, was essential, fundamental, while Martin tried to live his life without much concern for social classes and categories.

This boldness deeply offended Charles, and he would have liked to humiliate him for good, to make him recognize his inferiority. On the other hand, the failure of his attempted seduction made him more ill humored and gloomy.

One night, still ailing from his sickness, caused by spite and rage, Charles got out of bed, not being able to sleep, and went down to the dining room. He opened a window and looked outside. The sky was serene and clear. The moon whitened the branches of the apple trees, covered with the snow of their tiny flowers. The peach trees spread their branches, open like fans, full of cocoons, along the walls. Charles was inhaling the warm night air when he heard whispering and listened carefully.

His sister Catherine was speaking, from the window of her room, with someone in the garden. When Charles realized it was Martin, he felt a very sharp pain and a suffocating feeling of anger.

He was always to find himself confronted by Martin. It seemed that their destiny was to cross paths and clash.

Martin was telling Catherine, jokingly, about the wedding of Bautista and Ignacia in Zaro, about the banquet celebrated in the house of the French-Basque's father, about the speech of the mayor of the little town ...

Charles was growing weak with fury. Martin had prevented his conquest of Ignacia, and was, in addition, dishonoring the Ohandos by being his sister's sweetheart, speaking to her at night. What hurt Charles more than anything, although he would not admit it, what humiliated him deep in his soul, was Martin's superiority in going about heedless of classes, aspiring to everything and overcoming everything.

That street urchin was capable of getting ahead, prospering, becoming rich, marrying his sister, and considering all of this logical, natural ... It was unbearable.

Charles would have enjoyed conquering Ignacia, then abandoning her, strutting scornfully in front of Martin; and Martin got the best of him by taking Ignacia out of his reach and making love to his sister.

A tramp, a thief, had made sport of him, a rich gentleman, heir of a noble house! And what was worse, this was only the beginning, the commencement of his brilliant career.

Charles, mortified by his thoughts, did not pay attention to what they were saying; then he heard a kiss and, shortly afterward, the branches of a tree moving.

After this a man could be seen descending a tree trunk, crossing the garden, mounting the wall, and disappearing.

The window of Catherine's room was closing, and at the same time Charles drew his hand to his forehead thinking about the tremendous opportunity he had lost. What a superb moment to put an end to that man who was always in his way.

One shot, pointblank, and that weed would not grow any more, would have no more ambitions, would not try to break out of his class. If he killed him everyone would consider it a case of justifiable defense against a highwayman, against a thief.

The next day Charles looked for his father's double-barreled shotgun; he found it, secretly cleaned it, and loaded it with heavy buckshot. He hesitated in using cartridges, but since it was difficult to take aim at night, he decided on the heavy buckshot.

Neither that night nor the next did Martin appear; but four days later Charles heard him in the garden. The moon had not yet come out, and this saved the enamored highwayman. Charles, being impatient, when he heard the rustling of the leaves, aimed and fired.

With the powder-flash he saw Martin on the trunk of the tree and he fired again.

There was a woman's shriek and the sound of a body hitting the ground.

Charles's mother and the women servants, alarmed, came out of their rooms shouting, asking what was happening. Catherine, as pale as a ghost, was so filled with emotion she was speechless.

Agueda, Charles, and the women servants went out to the garden. Under the tree, on the ground and on the moist grass were several drops of blood, but Martin had escaped.

"Don't worry, miss," one of the servants said to Catherine. "Martin was able to get away."

Mrs. Ohando, who found out what had happened from her son, sought the advice of the priest Felix.

They tried to make Catherine understand the foolishness of the plan, but the girl was stubborn and was prepared to resist.

"Martin came to tell me about Ignacia, and since obviously he isn't wanted in here, he had to jump over the wall."

When Charles learned that Martin was only wounded in the arm and that he was going around town bandaged, being the hero, he felt furious; but he dared not go out on the street just in case he should meet him.

Because of the offense, the hostility between Charles and Catherine, which already existed, increased to such an extent that Agueda, in order to avoid bitter quarrels, sent Charles to Oñate again, and she devoted herself to watching over her daughter.

Part II

Wanderings and Excursions

Chapter 1

Concerning the Preliminaries to the Last Carlist War

THERE ARE MANY FOR whom life is exceptionally easy. They may be compared to a ball that rolls down an inclined plane, having no obstacles or any difficulty at all.

Is it talent, instinct, or luck? Their own associates assert that it is instinct or talent; their enemies call it chance or luck, and the latter is more probable than the former because there are men extremely well prepared for life, intelligent, energetic, strong, and who, nevertheless, only falter and stumble constantly.

A Basque proverb says: "Valor frightens away bad luck." And this is true at times … when you are lucky.

Zalacaín was fortunate; everything he attempted he did well. Business, smuggling, love, games … His main occupation was horse and mule trading; he bought them in Dax and smuggled them through Alduides or through Roncesvalles.

He had an associate named Capistun the American, a very intelligent, older man, whom everyone called the American, although it was known that he was a Gascon. He got his nickname from having lived in America for a long time.

Bautista Urbide, a former baker at the Archipi bakery, often participated in the expeditions. Both Capistun and Martin used the town of Zaro, next to San Juan de Pie de Puerto, where Ignacia lived with Bautista, as a resting point.

Capistun and Martin knew, as few did, the ports of Ibantelly and Atchuria, Alcorrunz and Larratecoeguia, the entire line of landmarks of Zugarra-murdi. They had often traveled the roads between Meaca and Urdax, between Izpegui and San Esteban de Baigorri, between Biriatu and Endarlaza, between Elorrieta, la Banca and Berdariz. In almost all the towns of the Basque-Navarrese border, from Fuenterrabia to Valcarlos, they had some agent for their smuggling business. They also knew, inch by inch, the paths on the slopes of Larrun Mountain, and they were thoroughly acquainted with the eastern side of Navarre, with those high meadows, located between the forests of Irati and Ori.

The life led by Capistun and Martin was tempestuous and dangerous. For Martin the watchword of old Tellagorri was the standard in his life. Whenever he found himself in a difficult situation, surrounded by carabineers; whenever he got lost on the mountain, in the middle of the night; whenever he had to make a great effort, he would remember the attitude and the voice of the old man when he said: "Firm! Always firm!" And he did what was necessary decisively at that moment.

Martin was cool and serene. He knew how to measure the danger and see the true situation of things, without exaggeration and without alarm. For business and for war man must be cold.

Martin was beginning to be imbued with French liberalism and to find his countrymen backward and fanatic; but in spite of this, he believed that the pretender Charles, the moment the war should start, would achieve victory.

In almost all southern France the same thing was believed.

The government of the Republic, the deputy-prefects and other public officials of the Spanish border allowed the rebels to pass; and in the coaches of Elizondo, through Alduides, San Esteban de Baigorri, and Añoa, the Carlist leaders traveled, with their command uniforms and insignia.

Martin and Capistun, besides the horses and mules, had taken weapons and materials necessary for the manufacture of gunpowder, cartridges and missiles to different parts of Guipúzcoa and Navarre, and they were able to bring a cannon left over from the Franco-Prussian War, sold by the French government, across the border.

The Carlist committees operated in the open. Generally, Martin and Capistun made their arrangements with the committee of Bayonne; but sometimes they had to deal with the one from Pau.

They had often left casks filled with weapons in the hands of young Carlists who were disguised as ox drivers. The Carlists loaded the casks on a cart and went into Spain.

"It's Rioja wine," they would say jokingly when they arrived at the towns, slapping the barrels, and the Mayor and secretary, who were accomplices, let them pass.

They would also load lead ingots, which were to be used to cast bullets, on carts which they covered with tiles.

The allusion to the impending war was noted in a number of indications and signs. Priests, Mayors and political leaders were preparing themselves. Often, when one went through a town, one could hear a shrill voice as in a festival shouting in Basque: "*Noiz zuazte?*" (When are you going?) Which meant: When are you going to the camp?

In Guipúzcoa they also sang a song in Basque that alluded to the war and that was called *Guguerá* (We are).

It went like this:

A Voice

Bigarren chandan
aditutzendet
ate joca, dan dan.
Ate onduan
norbait dago ta
galdezazu nordan.

(*For the second time I hear them knocking on the door, tap, tap.*
There's someone by the door. Ask who it is.)

Several Voices

Ta gu guerá,
ta gu guerá
gabiltzanac
gora berá
etorri nayean onerá.

Ta gu guerá,
ta gu guerá
Quirlis Carlos,
Carlos Quirlis,
escarri nayean onerá.

(*We are, we are the ones who go from top to bottom wanting to come here.*
We are, we are, Quirlis Charles, Charles Quirlis, wanting to bring you here.)

And while they were organizing and preparing themselves for a ferocious, bloody war in the provinces, in Madrid, politicians and orators were devoting themselves with enjoyment to fancy rhetorical exercises.

One day in May, Martin, Capistun, and Bautista went to Vera. Mrs. Ohando had a house in the district of Alzate and had gone to stay there a while.

Martin wanted to talk to his girlfriend, and Capistun and Bautista went with him. They left Sara and crossed a submerged pool until they came out of Lizuñaga, and from there to the district of Illecueta.

Martin relied on one of the Ohando servant women, who was friendly toward him, and she made it possible for him to speak to Catherine. While Martin stayed in Alzate, Capistun and Bautista went into Vera.

At that very time, the Bourbon pretender Charles was arriving surrounded by a staff of Carlist generals and some French Vendeans.

A patriotic speech was delivered, and then Charles, repeating the conclusion of the speech, exclaimed:

"Today, the second of May. A national holiday! Down with the foreigner!"

The foreigner was Amadeo of Savoy.

Capistun and Martin walked among the groups. It was said that one of those gentlemen was Cathelineau, the descendant of the famous Vendean general; they were also pointing out the Count of Barrot and a Navarrese marquis.

When Martin arrived at Vera the square was filled with Carlists; Bautista said to him:

"The war has begun."

Martin was deep in thought.

Martin, Capistun and Bautista returned to France by way of the irrigation ditch of Sara. Bautista shouted frequently, with irony in his voice: "Down with the foreigner!" Zalacaín was thinking about the course of events that that war which had just begun would take and about how it could influence his love affair with Catherine.

Chapter II

How Martin, Bautista and Capistun Spent a Night on the Mountain

ONE WINTER NIGHT THE three men were traveling with four magnificent mules loaded with huge bundles. Having left Zaro in the afternoon, they made their way toward the heights of Larrun Mountain. Following along the banks of a stream that descended to join the Nivelle, and crossing meadows, they reached a hut where they stopped to eat.

The three men were Martin Zalacaín, Capistun the Gascon, and Bautista Urbide. They were carrying a shipment of uniforms and overcoats.

The goods were to go to Lesaca where the Carlists would collect them.

After eating supper in the hut, the three men got the mules and continued their trip, ascending Larrun Mountain.

The night was cold and it was starting to snow. Their feet slipped on the roads and paths, which were full of mud; at times a mule would get into a pool of mud up to its belly and it took a great effort to free the animal.

The mules were carrying a lot of weight. They had to go the long way, without using the side paths, and the journey was becoming tedious. When they reached the top and got to the pass, a wind and snowstorm caught the travelers by surprise.

They were just at the border. The snow was becoming heavier; it was not easy to continue forward. The three men stopped the mules, and while Capistun stayed with them, Martin and Bautista separated to the sides to see if they could find some shelter, cabin, or shepherd's hut nearby.

Zalacaín saw a hut used by carabineers, which was closed up a short distance away.

"Hello! Anybody in there?" he shouted.

No one answered.

Martin pushed the door, which was secured with a nail, and entered the hut. He immediately ran to inform his friends of his discovery. The bundles that the mules were carrying included blankets, and by spreading them out and fastening them at one end on the hut of the carabineers and at the other end on some branches, they improvised a shed for the mules.

Once the freight and animals were safe the three men went into the house of the carabineers and lit a nice fire. Bautista quickly made a torch with pine fibers to light that obscure place.

They waited for the storm to pass and the three of them got ready to kill time by the fire. Capistun was carrying a gourd filled with Armagnac whiskey, and mixing it with water, which they heated, they all three drank.

Then, as was only natural, they spoke of the war. Carlism was spreading and gaining victory after victory. It was gradually making progress in Catalonia and in the Basque-Navarrese country.

The Spanish Republic was a calamity. The newspapers spoke of assassinations in Malaga, fires in Alcoy, soldiers disobeying their leaders and refusing to fight. It was a disgrace.

The Carlists seized a number of towns abandoned by the liberals. They had entered Estella.

On both shores of the Bidasoa, on the Spanish side as well as on the French, a great enthusiasm was felt for the cause of the Pretender.

Capistun and Bautista indicated their acquaintances who had enlisted in the uprising. For the most part they were young men but there were also some old ones. They began naming them.

Among them were John Echeberrigaray from Ezpeleta; Thomas Albandos from Añoa; the blacksmith Lerrumburo from Zaro; Echebarria from Irisarri; Galparzasoro the sandal maker from Urruña; Mearuberry the butcher from Ostabat; Michael Larralde the one from Azcain;

Carricaburo the lad from a settlement in Arhamus; Chaubandidegui the son of the confectioner from Azcarat; Peyrohade and Lafourchette the two young men from the marketplace of Hasparren.

"Brave rogues!" murmured Martin, who was listening.

Capistun and Bautista continued their enumeration. There were also Bordagorri the one from Meharin; Achucarro from Urdax; Etchehun the poet from Chacxu; Gañecoechia from Osses; Bishiño from Azparrain; Listurria from Briscus; Rebenacq from Pourtales; the landowner of Saint-Palais with Baron Lesbas d'Armagnac of Mauleon; Dechessary the sacristan of Biriatu; Guilbeleguieta from Barcus; Iturbide from Hendaya; Echemendi the miner from Articuza; Chocoa the stonecutter from San Esteban de Baigorri; Garraiz the pigeon hunter from Echalar; Setoain the woodsman from Esterensuby; Isuribere the shepherd from Urepel and Chiquierdi the one from Zugarramurdi.

The Basques, following the tendencies of their race, were going off to defend the old against the new. Thus they had fought in more remote times against the Romans, the Goths, the Arabs, the Castilians, always for old customs and against new ideas.

These villagers and old noblemen of Vasconia and Navarre, this peasant semi-aristocracy from both sides of the Pyrenees, believed in that common, foreign, naturalized Bourbon, and they were prepared to die to satisfy the ambitions of such a grotesque adventurer.

The French legitimists pictured him as a new Henry IV, and since it was from there, from Beam, that the Bourbons came out at another period to rule in Spain and in France, they dreamed that Charles VII would triumph in Spain, end the damned French Republic, give jurisdiction to Navarre, which would be the center of the world, and in addition reestablish the political power of the pope in Rome.

Zalacaín felt very Spanish, and he said that the French were a bunch of swine because they ought to make war in their own land, if they liked.

Capistun, as a good republican, affirmed that war was in all ways barbarian.

"Peace, peace is what we need," the Gascon added; "peace so we can work and live."

"Oh, peace!" replied Martin, contradicting him; "War is better."

"No, no," Capistun responded. "War is nothing but barbarism."

They debated the subject; the Gascon, being more intelligent, presented better arguments, but Bautista and Martin replied:

"Yes, all that is true; but war is also beautiful."

And the two Basques specified their idea of beauty. Deep inside both of them was a simple, heroic, juvenile and brutal dream. They saw themselves on the mountains of Navarre and Guipúzcoa leading a squad, always lying in ambush, in a continuous adaptability of will, attacking, fleeing, hiding in the shrubs, making forced marches, burning enemy villages.

And what rejoicings! What triumphs! Going into the towns on horseback, your cap over your eyes, your sword at your waist, while the church bells ring. Seeing, when you retreat from an overwhelming force, how the bell tower of the village where you have protection appears amidst the verdure of the farms; defending a trench heroically and planting your flag while the bullets whistle by; staying calm while the shells fall, exploding just a short distance away, and riding from one side of the road to the other in front of the squad while everyone marches in time with the drum…

What emotions those must have been! And Bautista and Martin dreamed about the pleasure of attacking and retreating, about dancing at the celebrations in the towns and about pillaging the city halls, about ambushing and escaping along damp trails and sleeping in a hut on a bed of dry grass…

"Barbarism! Barbarism!" replied the Gascon to all this.

"What barbarism!" Martin exclaimed. "Do you always have to be a slave, planting potatoes or taking care of pigs? I prefer war."

"And why do you prefer war? To steal."

"You shouldn't talk, Capistun, because you're a trader."

"So what?"

"So you and I steal with our account books. Between stealing on the road and stealing with an account book, I prefer those who steal on the road."

"If business were theft, there wouldn't be any society," the Gascon replied.

"So?" Martin said.

"So there wouldn't be any cities."

"As I see it cities are made by the wretched and are used as objects to be sacked by strong men," said Martin, violently.

"That is being an enemy of humanity."

Martin shrugged his shoulders.

A little after midnight the snow began to stop, and Capistun gave the order to leave. Stars had filled the sky. Their feet sank in the snow and there was a deadly silence.

"Sing, pals," said the Gascon, who was bothered by so much sadness and tranquility.

"Don't let them hear us," Bautista advised.

"Oh, no!" And the Gascon sang:

> *¡Oan! Oan lus de deuan,*
> *lus de darrer que seguirán.*
> *Lus de darrer, oan, oan,*
> *que seguirán a trot de can.*

(Forward! Forward those ahead and those behind who will follow. Those behind, who will follow at a dogtrot, forward, forward.)

This was an old Gascon song to measure the march; very good for the plains, but not very appropriate for those rough, out-of-the-way places.

Bautista, encouraged by the Gascon's example, sang a French-Basque *zortzico* that went like this:

> *Gau erdi da*
> *errico orenean*
> *iñon ez da*
> *arguiric lurrean*
> *ez diteque*

66

mendian adi deuzic
aicearen
arrabotza baicir.

(It is midnight on the town clock; nowhere is there any light shining on the ground; on the mountain you can only hear the noisy sound of the wind.)

Bautista's song was of a wild melancholy nature; Martin let out a shout, the "*irrintzi*," like a long outburst of laughter or a wild whinny, ending in a jeering laugh. Capistun, as if protesting, sang:

Del castelet a l'aube
sort Isabeu,
es blanquette sa raube
como la neu.

(Isabella leaves the little castle at dawn; her clothes are white as the snow.)

Martin and Bautista did not like the Gascon's songs because they seemed too sweet, and the Gascon did not like theirs either because he found them sinister. They debated the good points of their respective countries from the popular songs to the customs and the wealth.

It was just about dawn; they were getting very close to Vera when they heard several shots in the distance. "What's going on here?" they wondered.

A moment later they again heard shots and a distant ringing of bells.

"We'll have to see what it is."

They decided as the most practical plan that Capistun, with the four mules, should go back slowly to the hut of the carabineers where they had spent the night. If nothing was happening in Vera, Bautista and Zalacaín would return immediately. If they were not back in two hours, Capistun should cross the border and take refuge in France: in Ascain, in Sara, or wherever he could.

The mules again started the journey to the pass and Zalacaín and his brother-in-law began to descend the mountain in a straight line, jumping, sliding on the snow, trying to keep their balance. A half hour later they reached the street of Alzate, the gates of which were closed.

They knocked at a familiar inn. No one responded for a while and finally, the innkeeper, frightened, appeared at the door.

"What's going on?" Zalacaín asked.

"The band of the Priest is in Vera again."

Bautista and Martin knew about the reputation of the Priest and about his enmity with some Carlist generals, and they agreed that it was dangerous to bring the contraband to Vera or Lesaca as long as the cassocked leader's people were around there.

"Let's go warn Capistun right away," Bautista said.

"Okay, you go," replied Martin; "I'll catch up with you before too long; go on."

"What are you going to do?"

"I'm going to see if I can find Catherine."

"I'll wait for you."

Catherine and her mother lived in a magnificent house in Alzate. Martin knocked at the door, and to the servant, who knew him by this time, he said:

"Is Catherine home?"

"Yes… Come in."

He went into the kitchen. It was big, spacious and somewhat dark. Around the wide chimney mantel hung a smooth white cloth fastened with nails. A thick black chain, the end of which held a caldron, descended from the center of the mantel. On one side of the chimney there was a little stool made of stone on which there were three pails in a row with shiny iron hoops which made them look more like silver. On the walls were reddish-copper saucepans and all the kitchen utensils, from the frying pans and bread shovels to the warming pan, which was also hanging on the wall as an integral part of the kitchen implements.

That order seemed rather absurd and unusual in contrast to the confusion outside.

The maid had gone up the stairs and in a while Catherine came down, wrapped in a large cloak.

"Is it you?" she said, sobbing.

"Yes, what's wrong?"

Catherine, crying, told him that her mother was very ill, her brother had gone off with the Carlists, and that they wanted to put her in a convent.

"Where do they want to take you?"

"I don't know; it hasn't been decided yet."

"When you know, write to me."

"All right, don't worry. Now go, Martin, because my mother has probably heard us talking, and since she was aware of the shots fired a little while ago, she's very upset."

In fact, shortly afterward, they heard a weak voice crying out:

"Catherine! Catherine! Who are you talking to?"

Catherine gave Martin her hand, and he squeezed her in his arms. She put her head on his shoulder, and seeing that she was being called again, she went up the stairs. Zalacaín watched her absorbed in thought, and then he opened the door, closed it slowly, and when he was in the street, he encountered an unexpected sight. Bautista was arguing and shouting with three armed men who did not seem to be on very friendly terms with him.

"What's going on?" Martin asked.

What was simply going on was that those three individuals belonged to the band of the Priest and they had presented Bautista Urbide with this simple dilemma:

"Either join the band or become a prisoner and get a good beating as a bonus."

Martin was about to jump in to defend his brother-in-law when he saw five or six armed young men at one end of the street. Ten or twelve were waiting at the other end. With his quick instinct for grasping the situation, Martin realized that the only thing to do was to submit, and in Basque, pretending to be very jovial, he said to Bautista:

"What is this, Bautista? Didn't you want to join a band? Aren't we

Carlists? Well, now we're on time."

One of the three men, seeing how Zalacaín was expressing himself, exclaimed happily:

"Hey, all right! This guy is one of us. Come on, both of you."

This man was a tall, thin villager, wearing a ragged uniform and with a clay pipe in his mouth. He seemed to be the leader and they called him Luschia.

Martin and Bautista followed the armed youths; they went from Alzate to Vera and stopped at a house with a guard stationed at the door.

"Bring them down! Bring them down!" Luschia said to his men.

Four young men went to the porch and up the steps.

Meanwhile, Luschia asked Martin:

"You two, where are you from?"

"From Zaro."

"Are you French?"

Martin did not want to say he was not because he knew that saying he was French could protect him.

"Okay, okay," the leader murmured.

The four villagers of the band who had entered the house brought out two old men.

"Tie them!" said Luschia, the villager with the pipe.

They brought a snare drum and a cestus out to the street, and they tied the two old men.

"What have they done?" Martin asked one of the bandsmen who was wearing a striped cap.

"They're traitors," he answered.

The one was a schoolteacher and the other a former partisan of the Priest's guerrilla band.

When the two victims were tied and with their backs bare, the executioner, the young man with the striped cap, rolled up his sleeves and grabbed a stick.

The schoolteacher beggingly implored:

"But we are all together!"

The ex-guerrilla said nothing.

There was no appeal or mercy. With the first blow the teacher lost consciousness; the other man, the former lieutenant of the Priest, kept quiet and began to take the beating with a sinister stoicism.

Luschia began to speak with Zalacaín. The latter told him a number of lies. Among them he said that he himself had put away near Urdax, in a cave, more than thirty modern rifles. The man heard this, and from time to time, turning to the executioner of his orders, he would say in a twangy voice:

"¡Jo! ¡Jo!" ("Strike, strike.")

And the staff fell again on the naked backs.

Chapter III

About Some Resolute Men Who Formed the Band of the Priest

WHEN THE BEATING WAS finished Luschia gave the order to march and the fifteen or twenty men went on toward Oyarzun, along the road that passes by the Agonia slope.

The band divided into two groups; Martin was in the first and Bautista in the second.

None of the men in the band had a mean or frightening appearance. Most of them looked like the local country residents; almost all of them were wearing black clothes, small blue caps, and in place of boots some were wearing sheepskin sandals that wrapped around their legs.

Luschia, the leader, was one of the Priest's lieutenants, and he also was head of his black guard. Without a doubt he enjoyed the commanding officer's trust. He was tall, bony, slender, and lean and had a huge nose.

Luschia had the kind of face that always gave you the impression of seeing it from a profile, and he had a protruding Adam's apple.

He seemed to be a good person up to a certain point, ingratiating and jovial. He certainly considered the acquisition of Zalacaín and Bautista an asset, but he distrusted them and made them travel in separate groups, although not as prisoners, and he did not allow them to speak privately.

Luschia also had his second lieutenants: Praschcu, Belcha and the bugler from Lasala. Praschcu was a big, happy-go-lucky, red-faced young man with a long beard, and judging from the words he used, the only thing he ever thought about was getting plenty to eat and drink. On the road all he talked about was food, about the dinner they took away from the priest of such-and-such a town or from the schoolteacher somewhere else, about the roast lamb they ate in this village and the bottles of cider they found in a tavern. For Praschcu war was just a series of big meals and drinking sprees.

Belcha and the bugler from Lasala were with Bautista's group.

Belcha (the young Black) was so called because he was small and dark; the bugler from Lasala had a violet-colored scar ornamenting his forehead. His nickname was derived from his job as overseer, the man who gives the signal for the commencement and suspension of work with a horn.

The bandsmen arrived at Arichulegui, a mountain near Oyarzun, at midnight and they entered a hut next to the hermitage.

This hut was the Priest's den. There he kept his munitions.

The commander was not there. A reserve detachment of some twenty men was guarding the hut. Night soon fell. Zalacaín and Bautista ate a mess of beans and slept on a nice bed of dry hay.

Very early the next morning they both felt themselves being rudely awakened; they got up and heard the voice of Luschia:

"Move it! Let's go!"

It was still night; the squad got ready in a moment. At noon they stopped at Fagollaga, and at dusk they reached an inn near Andoain where they halted. They went into the kitchen. According to Luschia the Priest would be there.

In fact, shortly afterward, Luschia called Zalacaín and Bautista.

"Come in," he told them.

They climbed the wooden stairs to the attic and knocked on a door.

"Can we come in?" asked Luschia.

"Come on."

Zalacaín, despite the fact that he was firm, felt a slight chill go over his whole body, but he straightened up and entered the room smiling. Bautista was intending to protest.

"I'll do the talking," Martin said to his brother-in-law. "Don't you say anything."

A lantern provided light for the room, from the ceiling of which ears of corn were hanging, and two men were seated at a pine table. One of them was the Priest; the other, his lieutenant, an officer whose nickname was the Soapmaker.

"Good evening," said Zalacaín in Basque.

"Good evening," the Soapmaker replied pleasantly.

The Priest did not answer. He was reading a paper.

He was a chubby man, short rather than tall; he had ordinary features and seemed to be a little over thirty years old. His only dominant characteristic was the way he looked at people—threateningly, obliquely and harshly.

A few minutes passed before the Priest finally looked up and said: "Good evening."

Then he went back to his reading.

There was something in that whole scene that seemed to be an act prepared for the purpose of frightening the visitors. Zalacaín realized this, pretended to be indifferent and calmly kept his eyes on the Priest. The latter was wearing a black cap tilted over his forehead, as if he were afraid that someone would look into his eyes. He had a rather long, crudely shaped beard, short hair, a kerchief around his neck, a black jacket with all the buttons fastened and a club between his legs.

There was something in that man's enigmatic personality reminiscent of bloodthirsty killers and executioners; his reputation for being cruel and fierce was spreading throughout Spain. He was aware of this and probably proud of the fear that the mere mention of his name caused in people. Basically he was a miserable, hysterical, sickly devil who was convinced that he had a divine mission to perform. He was born, as the story went, in a gutter, in Elduayen; he had been ordained and received a parish in a small town near Toulouse. One day he was celebrating mass when they came to arrest him. The Priest gave them the excuse that he was just going to take off his church garments, and he jumped out a window, escaped and began to organize his band.

That sinister man was surprised by the coolness and serenity of Zalacaín and Bautista, and without looking directly at them, he asked:

"Are you two Basques?"

"Yes," said Martin, moving forward.

"What were you doing?"

"Smuggling weapons."

"For whom?"

"For the Carlists."

"What commission did you deal with?"

"Bayonne."

"What kind of guns did you bring?"

"Berdan and Chassepot."

"Is it true that you have weapons hidden near Urdax?"

"There and in other places."

"Who were they for?"

"The Navarrese."

"Fine. We'll go get them. If we don't find them we'll shoot you."

"Okay," said Zalacaín coldly.

"Go ahead," replied the Priest, annoyed because he had not intimidated his audience.

When they were leaving the Soapmaker approached them on the stairway.

He had a military appearance and he seemed friendly and well educated.

He had been a rural policeman.

"Don't be afraid," he said. "If everything goes as you say, nothing will happen to you."

"We aren't afraid of anything," Martin answered.

The three men went to the kitchen of the inn, and the Soapmaker mixed with the people from the band who were waiting for dinner to be served.

At the same table sat the Soapmaker, Luschia, Belcha, the bugler from Lasala, and a fat man they called Anchusa.

The Soapmaker refused to let Praschcu sit at his table because he said that if they allowed that barbarian to eat at the beginning he would not leave anything for the others.

Because of this a young man, an ex-seminarian named Dantchari and known also as the Student, who was a member of the band, remembered the song of Vilinch called the song of the "Porridge," and since it deals with a gluttonous priest, he had to sing it in an undertone so the commander would not hear it.

The innkeeper brought the dinner and a number of bottles of wine and cider, and since the trip from Arichulegui to where they were had sharpened their appetites, they attacked the food like starving animals.

They were eating when they heard a knock at the door.

"Who's there?" asked the innkeeper.

"Me. A friend," was the answer from outside.

"Who are you?"

"Ipintza the Madman."

"Come in."

The door opened and the old beggar came in wearing a loose-fitting brown coat with one of the sleeves tied in such a way that it could be used as a pocket. Dantchari the Student knew him and said that he sold songs for a living and that everyone thought he was crazy because he would sing and dance while reciting them.

Ipintza the Madman sat down at the table and the innkeeper gave him the leftovers from the dinner. Then he joined the group of bandsmen formed around the chimney.

"Wouldn't you like a song?" he said.

"What songs do you have?" the Student asked him.

"I have a lot. The one about the wife who complains about her husband, the one about the husband who complains about his wife, 'Pello Joshepe.'"

"Those are all old."

"I also have 'Hurra Pepito' and the master and servant song."

"That's a liberal song," said Dantchari.

"I don't know," Ipintza the Madman answered.

"What do you mean you don't know? I don't think you're completely orthodox."

"I don't know what that means. Wouldn't you like some songs?"

"Well, all right, give me an answer. Are you orthodox or heterodox?"

"I already told you I don't know what you mean."

"What do you think about the Trinity?"

"I don't know."

"What do you mean you don't know? And you have the nerve to say so? Where does the Holy Ghost come from? Does He come from the Father, or the Son or both? Or do you think His hypostasis is consubstantial with the Father's or the Son's?"

"I don't know anything about it. Would you like some songs? Wouldn't you like to buy some songs from Ipintza the Madman?"

"Oh! So you're not going to answer? Then you are a heretic. 'Anathema sit.' You are excommunicated."

"Me? Excommunicated?" said Ipintza, terrified and stepping back and raising high his white stick.

"Okay, okay," Luschia shouted to the Student. "That's enough fooling around."

Praschcu threw several armfuls of dry branches on the fire which gaily crackled; then some of the men began playing cards, and Bautista displayed his magnificent voice by singing several zortzicos.

Dantchari the Student challenged Bautista to a verse recitation contest, and he accepted the challenge. They both began with the refrain:

> *Orain esango dizut*
> *nic zuri eguia.*

> *(Now I'll tell you the truth.)*

And in their attempts to make rhymes they each composed a number of absurd and amusing lines which really pleased the audience.

They both deserved congratulations and applause. Then Dantchari affirmed that he could sing soprano, and with Bautista he sang the song that begins:

> *Marichu, ¿nora zuaz*
> *eder galant vi?*

> *(Mary, where are you going looking so pretty?)*

Bautista, singing the part of the boy, and Dantchari the part of the girl, asking each other questions and replying with jesting candor, absolutely delighted everyone.

Then Bautista sang the beautiful song of the country of Soul that goes like this:

> *Urzu churia errazu,*
> *nora yoaten cera zu.*
> *Ezpaniaco mendi guciac*
> *elurrez beteac dituzu.*
> *Gaur arratzean ostatu*
> *gure echean badezu.*

> *(White dove, tell me where you are going. All the mountains in Spain are covered with snow. If you want shelter tonight come to my house.)*

The bandsmen applauded; but they liked the preceding duet even more than this romantic song, and the Soapmaker, realizing this, bought a piece of paper from Ipintza the Madman which contained the lyrics of the new song of Vilinch called "Juana Vishenta Olave," written by the author who adapted it to a popular composition titled "Orra Pepito!"

The song of Vilinch was a love dialogue between the village landowner and a tenant's daughter, whom he is trying to seduce.

The Student put on a skirt belonging to the innkeeper's wife and tied a kerchief around his head. Bautista slipped on a high hat that someone found somewhere, and together they sang the candid duet of Vilinch. The noise got so loud that the singers had to quit because the Priest shouted from above that they were keeping him awake.

Everyone went to look for a place to sleep, and Martin said to Bautista in French:

"Stay alert, eh! We have to be ready to get away at the first opportunity."

Bautista nodded affirmatively, letting him know that he would not forget.

Chapter IV

The Almost Improbable Story of Joshe Cracasch

IT RAINED THE NEXT two days and the band remained at the inn, doing some reconnoitering around the area. Neither Zalacaín nor Bautista saw the Priest. Obviously he only appeared on important occasions.

It was only natural that so many inactive people should pass the time by the fire chatting and telling different episodes and adventures.

There was a very melancholy lad from Toulouse in the band whose only interests were looking at himself in a hand-mirror and playing the accordion. This young man's name was Joshe Cacochipi, and some of the men, behind his back, called him Joshe Cracasch, or its Spanish equivalent, José Manchas (Joe Stains).

Martin and Bautista asked him several times the reason for his being so sad, if he had tooth aches, indigestion, family problems or some bladder disorder. Cacochipi, alias Cracasch, would answer all these questions by saying that nothing was wrong with him, but he would sigh as if all those calamities were striking him at the same time.

Since this Cacochipi was such a mysterious person, Martin asked Dantchari the Student, because he was also from Toulouse, if he knew the story of his countryman and friend, and the ex-seminarian replied:

"If you say nothing to him, I'll tell you Joshe's story, but you must promise me not to make fun of him."

"We won't make fun of him or say anything to him."

Dantchari spoke in Spanish with that classical pedantry of priests

80

and seminarians who believe that for greater clarity it is indispensable to throw in from time to time some Latin word among people who are absolutely ignorant of that language.

"Well you must know," said Dantchari, "that Joshe Cacochipi, the youngest son of Andre Anthoni the confectioner, has always been known, *urbi et orbe,* by the nickname Joshe Cracasch.

"This nickname fitted him well because years ago and even months ago, Joshe was the most forsaken boy in the city and its outlying areas; consequently, the whole town, *nemine discrepante,* nicknamed him Cracasch.

"The only passion Joshe ever had, until very recently, was for music.

"They tried to make him study to be a priest and to get him ordained *in sacris,* but it was impossible.

"One might say that he is a musician *per se* and a man *per accidens.*

"For many years he spent eight and nine hours at the piano, doing exercises, and since his only interest was music he was terribly negligent with everything else.

"He would wear a suit covered with large grease spots, a dirty cap, long hair and forget to put on a tie. He was a real mess.

"Therefore they called him Joshe Cracasch, and not only did this nickname not offend him, but it seemed to please him; on the other hand, his mother, Andre Anthoni, really got angry when she heard that they were calling her son by that name.

"Nearly a year ago a wealthy man from America by the name of Arizmendi, who they say was a pirate…, I don't know, *relata refero,* arrived in town. As I say, this gentleman asked the parish priest:

"'What music teacher could I get for my boy?'

"'The best: Joshe Cacochipi,' answered the priest.

"They spoke to Cracasch and he shrugged his shoulders and said that it was all right with him. His mother got him some clean clothes and advised him to be careful with what he said and to be prudent since the position could be a *modus vivendi* for him. Cracasch promised to be very prudent.

"He arrived the first day at Arizmendi's house and asked for the master.

"It was a girl who opened the door and shortly afterward a gentleman appeared. The girl told him to leave his hat on the hanger.

"'Why?' replied Joshe. And then, addressing the gentleman, he asked: 'She's the servant, eh?'

"'No, this young lady is my daughter,' answered Mr. Arizmendi, coldly.

"Cracasch realized he had made a mistake and tried to correct it by saying:

"'She's very pretty. She surely does look a lot like you!'

"'No. She's my stepdaughter,' answered Mr. Ariz-mendi.

"'Ha ha…, that's funny!… She probably already has a boyfriend, eh?'

"Cacochipi touched upon a subject that was worrying the family since the girl was having a love affair with a cousin against the will of her parents.

"Mr. Arizmendi told him not to ask any more impertinent questions, that he already knew he was half-idiotic but that he should learn to compose himself.

"Joshe, very hurt at such abruptness, went to the boy's room where he gave his first solfeggio lesson. Those harsh words from Mr. Arizmendi surprised rather than offended him. Joshe was not at all a malicious person; he had spent his entire life thinking about music and he knew nothing about other things.

"The sadness of the father, the mother and the sisters displeased Cacochipi, who was invited several times to eat with the Arizmendi family, and he tried to cheer them up a little; because as the worldly man says: *Omissis cursis, jucunde vivendum esse,* which means that one should live happily and without cares.

"The first thing that occurred to Cracasch, one day when he imagined that he had gained the Arizmendi family's trust, was to imitate the sound of a train during dessert; then he tried to sing a song that was very popular at the tavern. In this song the singer pretends to be playing the flute and the bass drum and to be eating from a stew pan, and then he gets half undressed while he sings. Joshe thought that when he took off his jacket and vest the whole family would burst out laughing; however, the effect was just the opposite because Mr. Arizmendi, looking at him with anger in his eyes, said:

"'All right, Cacochipi, put your vest on and don't take it off again in front of us.'

"Joshe got cold and not exactly because he did not have his vest on.

"'Nothing pleases these people,' he murmured.

"One day he came to give his lesson with several beauty spots painted on his face and no one paid any attention; another day, aided by his pupil, he fastened the place settings to the table..., and nothing happened.

"'How's it going, Cracasch?' someone would ask him in the street. 'How is the Arizmendi family?'

"'Oh! They're people who don't like anything...' he would reply. 'You do nice things to amuse them..., and you get no response.'

"On the Shrovetide holiday Joshe Cracasch got one of his peculiar ideas, and it was to convince his pupil to take out some dresses belonging to his mother and one of his sisters. The two of them would put on the dresses and play a very funny joke on the Arizmendi family.

"'Now they are surely going to laugh,' Cacochipi was saying to himself.

"The boy wasted no time quibbling, and on Shrovetide Sunday he took the best dresses he could find and brought them to the confectioner's shop. Teacher and pupil put on the feminine apparel, and each carrying a broom, they went to the church door.

"When Arizmendi, his wife and his daughters came out from mass, Cacochipi and his pupil rushed at them and began squeezing and hitting them; Joshe reminded Arizmendi that he had false teeth, his wife that she had a hair-switch, and he reminded the oldest daughter about her boyfriend with whom she had quarreled. After mentioning some more things of this kind the two disguised fellows went jumping away.

"The next day, when he arrived at the Arizmendi house, Cracasch thought:

"'Sure, they're going to congratulate me for yesterday's joke.'

"He went in and it seemed that everyone looked serious. Suddenly Arizmendi came up to him and in a tone of voice that was more enraged than severe, in an awful *ab irato*, he said:

"'Don't ever set foot in my house again. Imbecile! If you weren't an idiot I'd kick you out.'

"'But why?' asked Joshe.

"'You still don't know, dummy? When one doesn't know how to behave like a human being one shouldn't have social contact with other people. I thought you were stupid, but not *that* stupid.'

"Cacochipi, for the first time in his life, felt offended. He locked himself in his house and began to think about Celedonia, Arizmendi's second daughter, and about her gentle voice and the *eloquendi suavitatem* with which she would greet him in the mornings, saying:

"'Good day, Joshe.'

"Cacochipi convinced himself that, as Arizmendi had said, he was stupid and that, besides, he was in love. These two convictions caused him to change his clothes, cut his hair, put on a new cap and not allow anyone to call him Cracasch.

"'Hey, Cracasch,' someone would say to him in the street.

"'Man! Did you call me Cracasch?' he would say.

"'Yeah, what about it?'

"'I don't want you to call me that again.'

"'But man, Cracasch…'

"'Here,' and Joshe would start throwing punches.

"In a short time Joshe got rid of his nickname of Cracasch. Celedonia Arizmendi had noted Joshe's transformation and she was aware of the part she was playing in this change. Joshe noticed that the girl was looking at him approvingly, but he was so shy that he would never have dared to say anything to her.

"Their love affair was about to become history before it had even started when the druggist's son decided to solve the whole problem.

"He wanted to have some fun with Joshe, and he wrote a comical love letter to Arizmendi's daughter, signing it 'Joshe Cracasch.'

"The girl sent the letter to Joshe telling him that someone was trying to make a fool of him but that she admired him and that he should come by her house so they could talk.

"Joshe went and saw the girl, said 'good afternoon,' and could not think of anything else to say; she asked him if his mother, Andre Anthoni, was well; he replied that she was, and then she said:

"'See you, Joshe.'

"'Goodbye.'

"Cacochipi seemed to be struck with astonishment; he needed to breathe, to get air, and he left Toulouse and took the road to Anoeta, passed Anoeta and then Irura and crossed Villabona and kept going and going until he ran across the band of the Priest, which was going to acquire glory *viribus et armis*. One of the bandsmen ordered him to halt and made him get down from the amatory-musical loftiness which had taken possession of him, presenting him with the simple dilemma of taking a beating or joining us.

"Joshe Cacochipi, notwithstanding his fondness for music, did not want anyone to 'play' on him and he has been with the band for a month already."

Such was the story of Joshe Cracasch as told by Dantchari the Student, with some additional Latin phrases not included by the author.

Chapter V

How the Band of the Priest Stopped the Coach Near Andoain

ON THE THIRD DAY at the inn the lack of activity was so great that the Soapmaker and Luschia agreed to stop the coach that went from San Sebastian to Toulouse that morning.

The men were stationed along the road in pairs; those farthest away would give the warning when the coach appeared and then fall back near the inn.

Martin and Bautista stayed with the Priest and the Soapmaker because the leader and his lieutenant did not trust them.

The warning came around 11:00 AM that the coach was arriving. The forward spies started going back toward the inn, sneaking along the sides of the road.

The coach was almost full. The Priest, the Soapmaker and the seven or eight men who were with them placed themselves in the middle of the road.

When the coach drew near the Priest raised his club and shouted:
"Halt!"

Anchusa and Luschia grabbed hold of the horses' bridle headstall and the coach stopped.

"Wow! The Priest!" exclaimed the coachman in a loud voice. "We've had it."

"Everybody out," the Priest ordered.

Egozcue opened the coach door. From inside the coach came a chorus of cries and screams.

"Come on! Get down and no noise," said Egozcue politely.

The first ones out were two Basque peasants and a priest; then came a man with blond hair, apparently a foreigner, followed by a young brunette who helped a fat lady with white hair get off.

"But, my word, where are they taking us?" exclaimed the fat lady.

No one answered her.

"Anchusa! Luschia! Unharness the horses," the Priest shouted. "Now everyone to the inn."

Anchusa and Luschia took the horses and only some eight men, including Bautista, Zalacaín and Joshe Cracasch, remained with the Priest.

"Take care of them," said the leader to two of his men, pointing to the peasants and the priest.

"You men," and he indicated Bautista, Zalacaín, Joshe Cracasch and two other armed men, "Go with the women and this traveler."

The fat lady, very upset, was crying.

"But are they going to shoot us?" she asked, groaning.

"Come on! Come on!" said one of the armed men, brutally.

The old lady knelt on the ground asking them to set her free.

The girl, pale, with her teeth clenched, had fire in her eyes. Doubtless she knew the procedures used by the Priest with women.

Sometimes he would strip them from the waist up, smear their breasts and backs with honey, and cover them with feathers; with some women he would cut their hair or smear it with tar and then stick it to their backs.

"Go on, ma'am," said Martin, "Nothing will happen to you."

"But where?" she asked.

"To the inn, not far away."

The young lady said nothing but looked at Martin with hatred and scorn.

The two women and the foreigner started walking along the road.

"Listen, Bautista," Martin said in French, "You take one, and I'll take the other. When they're not looking."

The foreigner, surprised, asked in the same language:

"What are you going to do?"

"Escape. We're going to take the rifles from those two. Help us."

The two armed men, when they heard them communicating in a language they did not understand, started getting suspicious.

"What are you talking about?" said one of them, stepping back and getting his gun ready.

He had no time to do anything because Martin hit him on the shoulder with a club and made him drop his rifle on the ground. Bautista and the foreigner struggled with the other one and took from him his gun and cartridges. Joshe Cracasch was not even aware of what was happening.

The two women, seeing that they were free, started running along the road toward Hernani. Cracasch followed them. He was carrying a defective shotgun which could be used as a last resort. The foreigner and Martin each had a rifle, but very few cartridges. They had been able to get a cartridge box from one of the men, but the other one raced off to tell the other bandsmen before they could get to him.

The foreigner, Martin, and Bautista ran and caught up with the two women and Joshe Cracasch.

They had a big advantage but the women could not run too fast; on the other hand, the Priest's men, in no time at all, would overtake them.

"Come on! Cheer up!" Martin was saying. "We'll be there in an hour."

"I can't," groaned the old lady. "I can't go on any more."

"Bautista!" exclaimed Martin. "Run to Hernani, find some men, and bring them back here. We'll stay and set up a defense for a while."

"I'll go," said Joshe Cracasch.

"All right, but leave the gun and ammunition."

The musician threw down his gun and cartridge pouch and started running as if possessed by the devil.

"I don't trust that silly musician," Martin murmured. "You go, Bautista. The pity is that we have an extra gun and no one to use it."

"I'll shoot," said the girl.

They got ready to face the enemy because they could hear the bandsmen coming.

Bullets were whizzing overhead. A little white cloud came into view at the same time as a bullet shot over the heads of the fugitives. The foreigner, the girl and Martin each took cover behind a tree and they divided the cartridges. Martin advised the old lady, who was still sobbing, to lie face-down on the grass.

"Are you a good marksman?" Zalacaín asked the foreigner.

"Me? Yeah. Not bad."

"And you, Miss?"

"I've fired a gun a few times too."

Six men, some one hundred yards from where Martin, the girl, and the foreigner were hiding, were gradually sneaking closer and closer. One of them was Luschia.

"I'm going to cripple that guy for life," said the foreigner.

And, in fact, he fired and one of the men fell to the ground screaming.

"Good shot," said Martin.

"Not bad," replied the foreigner, coldly.

The other five men went to pick up their wounded companion and brought him to safety. Then four of them, led by Luschia, fired at the tree from behind which the shot had come. They doubtless believed that Martin and Bautista were positioned there, and they slowly started closing in on the tree. Then Martin fired a shot and wounded one of them in the hand.

Now there were only three able to fight, and retreating and taking cover behind trees, they continued shooting.

"Do you think your mother has rested enough?" Martin asked the girl.

"Yes."

"Then let her get out of here. And you go with her."

"No, no."

"We can't lose any time," shouted Martin, stamping the ground with his foot. "She goes alone or with you. Get going! Right now."

The girl left Martin the gun and started down the road with her mother.

Martin and the foreigner waited; then without shooting they began to retreat until, when they reached a turn in the road, they started running as fast as their legs could carry them. They soon caught up to the old lady and her daughter.

The race ended a half hour later when they heard the bullets whizzing over their heads again.

There were no trees around behind which to take cover, but there were some piles of crushed stone used for road construction, and Martin and the foreigner spread out and got down under the protection of these stone piles. The old lady and her daughter threw themselves on the ground.

Soon several men appeared; obviously none of them wanted to attack, and they got the idea of surrounding the fugitives and catching them in a crossfire.

Four of them took a short cut through the cornfields on one side of the road while four others advanced along the other side where there were some apple trees.

"If Bautista doesn't get here with some men pretty soon, we're really going to be in trouble," Martin exclaimed.

The old lady, when she heard this, started moaning again and grieving about the fact that she had escaped.

The foreigner took out his watch and muttered:

"He had enough time. He must not have found anyone."

"That must be it," said Martin.

"Let's try to fight back as best we can," replied the foreigner.

"Fine chance we have!" Martin mumbled.

"The truth is that there is a fine chance to do a lot of things, even to shoot somebody."

"In that case we'll have to make sure it's not us who get shot, if we can."

Two or three bullets whizzed by and hit the ground.

"Surrender!" said the voice of Belcha from behind the apple trees.

"Come and get us," shouted Martin, and he saw one of them aiming at him from a hill, near a tree; he also took aim and the two shots were fired almost simultaneously. Moments later the man appeared again, this time closer, hiding behind some ferns, and he shot at Martin.

Zalacaín felt something strike his thigh and realized that he was wounded. He put his hand on the wound and felt something warm. It was blood. With his hand stained with blood he grabbed his gun, and propping himself up on the stones, he aimed and fired. Then he felt his strength being sapped because he was losing so much blood, and he fainted.

The foreigner waited a moment; but just then a company of local infantrymen could be seen coming down the road running and shooting, and the Priest's men retreated.

Chapter VI

How Miss Briones Took Care of Martin Zalacaín

When Martin Zalacaín again realized that he was alive, he found himself in a bed, surrounded by thick curtains.

He made an effort to move and felt very weak, with a slight pain in his thigh.

He vaguely remembered what had happened, the fight on the road, and he tried to find out where he was.

"Hey!" he shouted in a weak voice.

The curtains opened and a brunette with dark eyes appeared.

"Finally. You are awake!"

"Yes. Where am I?"

"I'll tell you the whole story later," said the brunette.

"Am I a prisoner?"

"No, no; you are safe here."

"In what town?"

"Hernani."

"Oh! Well. Couldn't you open those curtains for me?"

"No, not just yet. The doctor will be here soon and if he finds that you are well, we'll open the curtains and let you talk. So now go back to sleep."

Martin felt lightheaded, and it was not very difficult for him to follow the girl's advice.

At noon the doctor arrived and he examined Martin's wound, took his pulse and said:

"Now he can start eating."

"And can we let him talk, doctor?" asked the girl.

"Yes."

The doctor left and the girl with the dark eyes drew the curtains, and Martin found himself in a large room with a rather low ceiling. The golden rays of the winter sun were shining through the windows. Moments later Bautista appeared in the room, on tiptoe.

"Hi, Bautista!" said Martin, mockingly. "How did you like our first war adventure, eh?"

"Oh, man! For me it was all right," the brother-in-law answered. "For you it probably wasn't too nice."

"Pshaw! We got out of it."

The girl with the dark eyes, whom Martin did not recognize at first, was the same one the Priest's men had ordered out of the coach and who later had escaped with them, accompanied by her mother.

This young lady told Martin how they had brought him to Hernani and removed the bullet.

"And I was not aware of any of this," said Martin. "How long have I been in bed?"

"You have had a very high fever for four days."

"Four days?"

"Yes."

"That's why I'm so weak. And your mother?"

"She too was ill, but she's up now."

"I'm very glad. You know? It's strange," said Martin, "you don't seem to be the same girl who came with us on the road."

"No?"

"No."

"And why?"

"Your eyes were sparkling in such an unusual and harsh way…"

"And not now?"

"Not now; now your eyes seem very gentle."

The girl blushed, smiling.

"The truth is," said Bautista, "you have been lucky. This young lady has taken care of you like you were a king."

"How could I do less for one of our rescuers?" she exclaimed, hiding her embarrassment. "Oh, but don't talk so much! This is too much for the first day."

"Just one question," Martin added.

"Go ahead," she replied.

"I'd like to know your name."

"Rose Briones."

"Thank you, Miss Rose," he murmured.

"Oh! Don't call me Miss. Call me Rose or Rosie, as they do at home."

"But I'm not a nobleman," Martin responded.

"Well if you aren't a nobleman, who can be?" she added.

Martin felt flattered and since Rose indicated, with her finger on her lips, that he should not talk any more, he closed his eyes.

Martin's condition improved very quickly; so quickly, that it seemed to him that he got better too soon.

When Bautista saw that his brother-in-law was about ready to get out of bed and that he was in good hands, as he said somewhat ironically, he left for France to join Capistun and carry on the business.

For Martin, Hernani was a veritable Capua, a spiritual Capua.

Rosie Briones and her mother, Josephine, pampered and flattered him.

If he had known it Martin could have recited, referring to himself, the old ballad of Lancelot:

> *Never was there a knight*
> *by ladies so well attended*
> *as was Sir Lancelot*
> *when from his village he wended.*

During the period of convalescence Rosie had long conversations with Martin. She was from Logroño where she lived with her mother. Actually it was Josephine's fault that the two women got involved in that terrible adventure. She had the idea of going to Villabona to see her son, whom they had been told lay wounded there. Fortunately, the report was not true.

Josephine, Rosie's mother, was a romantic woman with foolish ideas. She adored her son, was very afraid that something would happen to him, but in spite of everything she had wanted him to be a soldier. When the adventure that ended in the stopping of the stagecoach was decided, and when she heard the remarks her daughter made about the unfortunate plan, she had replied:

"The Carlists are Spaniards and gentlemen and they cannot do harm to a couple of ladies."

In spite of this impossibility they had been on the verge of being tarred and feathered or beaten by the Priest's men.

Martin became convinced that the good lady stubbornly refused to look at things realistically. She saw everything in her own way and she convinced herself that things were as she had imagined them. If it might be said that the mother was scatterbrained, the same thing could not be said about her daughter. Unlike most girls she was clever and lively and her judgment was quick, sound and clear.

To amuse the patient Rose often read to him novels by Dumas and poems by Bécquer. Martin had never before heard poetry and he was very impressed; but what amazed him most of all was the wisdom of Rosie's commentaries. Nothing escaped her.

Soon Martin was able to get up and, limping, walk around the house. One day when he was telling of his life and adventures, Rosie suddenly asked him:

"And Catherine, who is she? Is she your sweetheart?"

"Yes. How do you know that?"

"Because you talked a lot about her while you were unconscious."

"Oh!"

"And is she pretty?"

"Who?"

"Your sweetheart."

"Yes, I think so."

"What? You only *think* so?"

"The fact is that I have known her since I was a boy and I'm so accustomed to seeing her that I hardly know what she's like."

"But aren't you in love with her?"

"I don't know, to tell the truth."

"How strange! What does she look like?"

"Well, you know…, a little blonde…"

"And does she have beautiful eyes?"

"Not as beautiful as yours," replied Martin.

Rose Briones' eyes flashed and she stared at Martin with one of her enigmatic looks.

One afternoon Rosie's brother came to Hernani. He was a courteous, attentive, but not very talkative young man. Josephine presented Zalacaín to her son as a savior, a hero.

The next day Rosie and her mother went to San Sebastian, to go from there to Logroño.

Martin went with them and their farewell was very affectionate.

Josephine hugged him and Rosie shook his hand several times and told him imperiously:

"Come and see us."

"Yes, I will."

"But do really come."

Rosie's eyes contained a world of promises.

When the mother and daughter left, Martin seemed to awaken from a dream; he remembered his business, his life and without losing any time, he headed for France.

Chapter VII

How Martin Zalacaín
Sought New Adventures

ONE WINTER NIGHT IT was raining in the streets of San Juan de Luz; an occasional lamp would tremble, blown by the wind, and from the doors of the taverns came voices and the sounds of accordions. In Socoa, which is the port of San Juan de Luz, in a tavern frequented by sailors, four men were sitting at a table, chatting. From time to time one of them would open the tavern door, walk silently out to the pier, look out toward the sea, and when he returned he would say:

"Nothing. *La Fleche* still isn't coming."

The wind was whistling in furious gusts over the black night and sea, and the sound of the waves lashing the wall of the pier could be heard.

In the tavern Martin, Bautista, Capistun and an old man whom they called Ospitalech were talking; they were talking about the Carlist War, which continued, unresolved, like a chronic illness.

"The war is coming to an end," said Martin.

"You think so?" asked old Ospitalech.

"Yes, things are going badly and I'm glad," added Capistun.

"No, there's still hope," Ospitalech replied.

"The bombardment of Irun was a total failure for the Carlists," said Martin. "And what hopes all those French legitimists had! Even the brothers of the Christian Gospel had given their children a vacation so that they could go to the border to see the spectacle. Scoundrels! And there we saw that arrogant pretender, Charles, with his horrible battalions, firing shell after shell, only to have to get out of there and run off toward Vera."

"If the war is lost we'll be ruined," Ospitalech muttered.

Capistun was calm; he intended to go back to live in his own country. Bautista, with the profits from the smuggling business, had extended his property. Of the three, Zalacaín was the only one not satisfied. If the thought of finding Catherine had not kept him going, he would have gone off to America.

He had learned nothing about his girl in over a year now; in Urbia no one knew anything of her whereabouts, and the rumor was being spread that Agueda had died, but it was just an unconfirmed rumor.

Of these four men in the Socoa tavern, the two who were satisfied, Bautista and Capistun, were chatting; the other two were filled with rage and silently looking at each other. Outside it was raining and the wind was blowing.

"Would one of you like to get involved in a rough deal where you'd have to risk your neck?" Ospitalech suddenly asked.

"Not me," said Capistun.

"Me either," Bautista replied distractedly.

"What's it about?" asked Martin.

"It's about penetrating the Carlist ranks and getting several generals, including Charles himself, to sign some drafts."

"Wow! That won't be easy," exclaimed Zalacaín.

"I know but it would pay well."

"How much?"

"The boss said he would give twenty percent to the man who brought him the signed drafts."

"And how much are the drafts worth?"

"How much? I don't know for sure how much they're worth. But you mean you'd go?"

"Why not? If I can make a lot…"

"Well wait a minute. I think the boat's coming; we'll talk about it later."

As a matter of fact, a shrill whistle had sounded breaking the silence of the night. The four men went out to the port, and the sound of the water being stirred by a screw propeller was heard, and then some sailors appeared on the steps of the pier and tied the cable to a post.

"Hello! Manisch," shouted Ospitalech.

"Hello!" was the answer from the sea.

"Everything all right?"

"Everything's all right," replied the voice.

"Good, let's go in," Ospitalech added, "because it's a miserable night."

The four men went back into the tavern, and shortly afterward Manisch, the skipper of the ship *La Fleche,* who took off his sea coat when he came in, and two other sailors joined them.

"So you're ready to take over this affair?" Ospitalech asked Martin.

"Yes."

"Alone?"

"Alone."

"Good, let's go to sleep. In the morning we'll go see the boss and he'll tell you what you can make."

The sailors of *La Fleche* began to drink, and one of them was singing, amid shouts and kicks, the song of *Les matelots de la Belle Eugenie.*

Martin got up very early the next day and took the train for Bayonne with Ospitalech. The two went to the house of a Jew named Levi-Alvarez. He was a very short man, half blond, half gray, with a curved nose, a white mustache and gold spectacles. Ospitalech worked for Mr. Levi-Alvarez and he told his boss how Martin was willing to offer his services for the difficult mission of entering the Carlist camp and bringing back the signed drafts.

"How much do you want for doing it?" asked Levi-Alvarez.

"Twenty percent."

"My gosh! That's a lot."

"Okay, no more talk; I'm leaving."

"Wait. Do you know that the drafts amount to a hundred twenty thousand dollars? Twenty percent would be an enormous figure."

''That's what Ospitalech offered me. That or nothing."

"What audacity! You have no consideration …"

"It's my last word. That or nothing."

"All right, all right. Agreed. Do you know that if you're lucky you're going to earn twenty-four thousand dollars?"

"And if I'm not, I'll be shot."

"Right. Do you accept?"

"Yes, sir, I accept."

"Good. Then we are agreed."

"But I demand that you make this contract formal by putting it in writing," said Martin.

"I have no objection."

The Jew was a little perplexed, and after hesitating a while, he asked:

"How do you want me to make it?"

"In promissory notes of a thousand dollars each."

The Jew, after hesitating, filled out the promissory notes and put on the seals.

"If you get them," he advised, "you can go ahead and send me the drafts from each town."

"Couldn't I deposit them with the notary of the towns?"

"Yes, that's better. A bit of advice: In Estella, don't go where the Minister of War is. Go to the general-in-chief and give him the letters."

"I'll do that."

"Then goodbye and good luck."

Martin went to the house of a Bayonne notary, asked him if the promissory notes were in order, and having been told that they were, he deposited them under receipt.

The same day he left for Zaro.

"Keep this paper for me," he said to Bautista and his sister, giving them the receipt. "I'm going away."

"Where are you going?" asked Bautista.

Martin explained to him his plans.

"That's crazy," said Bautista. "They'll kill you."

"No way!"

"Any of the Priest's men who see you will turn you in."

"There aren't any of them in Spain. Most of them are around Buenos

Aires. Some of them are here, in France, working."

"It doesn't matter; what you are planning to do is just crazy."

"Man! I'm not forcing anyone to come with me," Martin retorted.

"Well if you think you're the only one who can do that, you're mistaken," replied Bautista. "I can go where anyone else can."

"I don't say you can't."

"But you seem to doubt it."

"No, man, no."

"Yeah, yeah, and to prove my point I'm going with you. It won't be said that a French-Basque doesn't dare go where a Spanish-Basque goes."

"But man, you're married," Martin responded.

"It makes no difference."

"Well, I can see that you want to go with me. We'll go together and if we succeed in bringing back the signed drafts I'll give you something."

"How much?"

"We'll see."

"What a rogue you are!" exclaimed Bautista. "Why do you want so much money?"

"How do I know? We'll see. I've got some things going through my head. What? I don't know but I'm good for something. It's an idea that I've had for a little while."

"What the hell kind of ambition do you have?"

"I don't know, boy, I don't know," Martin answered; "but there are people who think of themselves as an old pot that can be used as a cup as well as a spittoon. Not me; I feel deep down, here inside, something hard and strong…; I can't explain it."

Bautista was puzzled over this obscure ambition that Martin felt because he was open and organized and he knew very well what he wanted.

They dropped this topic and spoke of the journey that they had to take.

It would begin by going in the little steamboat *La Fleche* to Zumaya and continuing from there to Azpeitia; from Azpeitia to Toulouse, and from Toulouse to Estella. Bautista, who had an excellent memory, memorized the list of names of all the people they had to see so that they would not have to carry the list with them and consult it in every place, which might get them into a compromising situation; they sewed the drafts between the leather of their leggings, and at night they boarded the ship.

They got on *La Fleche* in Socoa and set out to sea. Bautista and Zalacaín spent the crossing in a small cabin, being tossed around. At dawn the pilot saw what seemed to him to be a war ship in the direction of the Cape of Machichaco, and picking up steam entered Zumaya.

Several Carlist Companies went out to the port ready to commence firing, but when they recognized the French ship they calmed down. After disembarking Bautista recalled, with the aid of his amazing memory, the names of the people they had to visit in this town. There were three or four merchants. They found them, had them sign the drafts, bought two horses, negotiated for a passport, and in the afternoon, after eating, they took the Cestona road.

They passed by the little town of Oiquina, composed of several rows of houses situated on the banks of the Urola River; then they passed Aizarnazabal, and at the Iraeta inn, near the bridge, they stopped to eat supper.

Night soon fell. Martin and Bautista ate and debated whether it would be better to stay there or go on, and they decided to continue.

They mounted their nags and as they started to go they saw a coach pulled by four horses leaving a house near the Iraeta bridge. The coach began to ascend the Cestona road with the horses trotting. This stretch of road, from Iraeta to Cestona, passes between two mountains with the river at the bottom. Especially at night this particular place is gloomy and treacherous.

Martin and Bautista, because of that feeling of brotherhood that one gets on lonely, deserted roads, tried to overtake the coach and talk to the driver, but obviously the driver had reasons for not wanting company because when he noticed he was being followed, he put the horses at a gallop and then urged them on faster.

Thus, with the coach ahead and Martin and Bautista behind, they went up to Cestona; and when they got there the coach made a quick turn and moments later a package fell to the ground.

"It's some smuggler," said Martin.

In fact, it was a smuggler; they spoke to him and the man confessed that he had been prepared to shoot them when he saw them pursuing him. The three went to the inn, having become friends, and Martin went to see a Carlist confectioner on *Mayor* street.

They slept at the Blas inn and very early in the morning Zalacaín and Bautista got ready to continue on their way.

The day was rainy and cold; the yellowish road, spotted with deep holes, twisted through green fields; Mt. Itarroiz, wrapped in mist, could not be seen. The river, which had risen, was a dark yellow color. They stopped at Lasao on the property of a Carlist baron to get the administrator to sign a document, and then they continued the windward course along the Urola up to Azpeitia.

The work there was rather difficult and it took them a while to finish what they had to do. By dusk they were free and since they preferred not to stay in large towns, they took a trail that ascended Mt. Hernio and slept in a village called Regil.

On the third day they took the Vidania road and reached Toulouse where they stayed a few hours.

From Toulouse they went to a nearby town to sleep. They were told that there was a band around there and they preferred to keep going. A few days before, this band had brutally beaten some girls because they had refused to dance with several of those highwaymen.

They left the town and, at times trotting, at times walking, they arrived at Amezqueta, where they stopped.

Chapter VIII

Several Anecdotes About Ferdinand of Amezqueta and the Arrival at Estella

IN AMEZQUETA THEY WENT to the inn next to the pelota court. It was cold and raining and they huddled up by the fire.

Among those at the inn was a witty rustic who began to tell stories. When two other rustics came into the kitchen he took out his big checked handkerchief and began hitting the tables and chairs with it as if he were chasing away flies.

"What's going on?" Martin asked him. "What are you doing?"

"It's these annoying flies," the rustic answered, seriously.

"But there aren't any flies here."

"Oh yes there are," the man replied, taking another swat with his handkerchief.

The innkeeper, laughing, pointed out to Martin and Bautista that since there were so many male flies in Amezqueta, they jokingly called the townsmen *euliyac* (the flies) and that therefore that funny character was brushing the tables and chairs with his handkerchief when two Amezquetans entered.

Martin and Bautista laughed and the rustic told a number of stories and anecdotes.

"I don't know how to tell anything," the man said several times. "If only I were *Perdinand!*"

"And who was *Perdinand?*" questioned Martin.

"Haven't you fellows ever heard about Perdinand of Amezqueta?"

"No."

"Oh! Well he was the funniest man in this whole district. The things that man used to tell!"

Martin and Bautista urged him to tell one of Ferdinand's stories, but the rustic was very reluctant because he affirmed that hearing him tell these amusing tales would only give a pale idea of the utterances of Ferdinand. However, at the insistence of the two, the rustic told this anecdote in Basque:

"One day Ferdinand went to the house of the parish priest of Amezqueta, who was a friend of his and who frequently invited him to dinner. When he came in the house he nosed around the kitchen and saw that the housekeeper was cleaning two trout: one, beautiful, weighing at least four pounds, and the other, tiny, with hardly any flesh. Ferdinand went to find the priest who, as usual, invited him to stay for dinner. The priest and Ferdinand sat down at the table. They were brought two kinds of soup and Ferdinand ate both; then came the stew, followed by a platter of cabbage with blood pudding, and when they got to the main course Ferdinand discovered that instead of serving the large trout, the damned housekeeper had served the small one, which had nothing on it but a spine.

"'Man, trout!' exclaimed Ferdinand. 'I'm going to ask it a question.'

"'What are you going to ask it?' said the priest laughing, expecting a joke.

"'I'm going to ask it if it has ever heard anything from the other fish it has known about my relatives on the other side of the ocean, in America. Because these trout know a lot.'

"'Oh, yeah, ask it.'

"Ferdinand picked up the platter with the trout on it and placed it in front of himself; then he put his ear close to the platter very seriously and listened.

"'What is it? Is it answering?' asked the priest's housekeeper, mockingly.

"'Yes, it's answering, it's answering.'

"'And what does it say? What does it say?' asked the priest.

"'Well it says,' answered Ferdinand, 'that it is very little, but that out there, in that pantry, there is a very large trout which probably knows more about my relatives.'"

A girl in the kitchen, when she heard the anecdote, burst out with a shrill laughter and started everyone else laughing.

Martin and Bautista also laughed with pleasure at the joker's technique; but the rustic affirmed that he had no knack for telling these stories.

They urged him to continue and the man told another tale about *Perdinand.*

"Another time," he said, "he went to Idiazabal where there was a pelota match and he arrived late at the inn, when everyone was already seated. The owner said to him:

"'There isn't any room for you, Ferdinand, nor probably will there be any food.'

"'Bah!' he replied. 'If you just give me what's left over for free!'

"'Well, sure, everything that's left over for you.'

"Ferdinand walked around the dining room.

"The two teams that had played pelota had sat down in separate groups at the round table. Ferdinand, seeing that they were brought legs of lamb on a platter, said to two or three of them in a whisper:

"'I don't know where the owner gets such beautiful, meaty dog legs.'

"'What? Dog legs?' they exclaimed.

"'Yes, dog legs; but don't tell those fellows; let them get sick.'

"'But no kidding, Ferdinand?'

"'Yeah, man; I saw the head myself in the kitchen. It was such a pretty poodle!'

"Having said this he left the dining room and when he returned they had a serving of rabbit. He went to the other end of the table and said to the opposing team:

"'What nice cats this innkeeper buys from the carabineers!'

"'Oh, but is this cat?'

"'Yes; don't tell those fellows, but I saw the tails in the kitchen.'

"A short time later Ferdinand was eating alone and he had plenty of rabbit and lamb. At dusk they all left the town a little drunk, and someone stopped along the way to vomit.

"'It's the dog that has made him sick,' some were saying, jokingly.

"'It's the cat,' the others were saying.

"And no one would say that it was the wine.

"'Friends,' said Ferdinand, 'when one eats both cat and dog, nothing happens. They fight inside you like cats and dogs but they don't bother you.'"

The girl with the shrill laugh again burst out and the rustic began to tell another anecdote, saying:

"The way Ferdinand ruined the marriage of a rich shoemaker from Toulouse and a girl friend of his wasn't bad either."

"Tell us, tell us," everyone said.

"Well, Ferdinand was serving as apprentice in the shoeshop of the late Ichtaber, Flat-nose from Toulouse, and I don't know if you know this, but Ichtaber was a very rich old shoemaker. Ferdinand had a very pretty girl friend, but Ichtaber the Flatnose, when he saw her, began to court her and to ask her to marry him, and since he was rich she accepted his proposal. The girl and the old man usually met in the shoeshop, and sly old Ichtaber, to feel more at ease, would send Ferdinand, using whatever pretext, to the back room. He acted as if he weren't annoyed, but he got his revenge. He went to see his girl friend and talked to her.

"'Yes,' he told her. 'Ichtaber is a good person and a wealthy man, it's true; but since he's a shoemaker and flat-nosed and has worked with leather all his life, he smells very bad.'

"'Liar!' she exclaimed.

"'No, no; observe for yourself. You'll see.'

"Ferdinand went to the shoeshop, grabbed a large bellows and filled it up with that residue that's left after tanning leather and that has a nauseating smell; then he made a hole in the thin wall of the back room and he waited for the right moment. In the afternoon the girl arrived and Ichtaber said to his apprentice:

"'Listen, Ferdinand, go to the back room a while and fix up those lasts that are in the box.'

"Ferdinand left and took the bellows. He looked through the hole. Ichtaber was kissing the girl's hand; then he aimed the bellows at her and shot a foul-smelling current of air through the hole in the thin wall. When Ferdinand next looked through the hole, he saw Ichtaber the Flat-nose with his hand clenching his little nostrils, and the girl doing the same.

"Then Ferdinand continued working the bellows at intervals until he got tired.

"Two days later the girl came again and the same thing happened; and then she didn't return any more because she said that Ichtaber the Flat-nose smelled like a corpse.

"Ichtaber courted another girl, but Ferdinand played the same trick with the bellows on him, and the shoemaker would say to his friends:

"'Wow! In my time things were different; girls were wholesome. Nowadays they all smell like dogs.'"

Again the gay, harsh laughter of the girl rang out.

The others who were present celebrated the roguish actions of Ferdinand of Amezqueta and then went off to bed.

The next morning Martin and Bautista left Amezqueta and followed a trail to Ataun, the place where Dorronsoro, the Carlist civilian leader, had been a public clerk.

On the way they met a boy from this town who was going to Echarri-Aranaz, and with him they went along a trail that followed the Aralar Mountain Range.

The three spoke of the progress of the war and the boy told an anecdote about Dorronsoro that was rather amusing. A young gentleman from San Sebastian, from a Carlist family, being what they used to call tinsmiths, who was very fat and bright, had come to him.

"'Look, sir,' he had said to the clerk, 'I am a very avid Carlist and my family is also; I should like to serve Charles, but as you can see I am not inclined to going around the hills, and I would like to get into some office work.'

"'Okay, I'll see if I can find something for you,' Dorronsoro told him. 'Come back tomorrow.'

"The young gentleman returned the next day and asked:

"'Well, have you found anything?'

"'Yes, I realize that you can't go out to the hills, so you'll go to work in the office… and you'll pay three pesetas a day.'"

Martin and Bautista praised Dorronsoro's decision. That night they reached the Araquil valley and stopped at Echarri-Aranaz. They went into the kitchen at the inn to warm up by the fire. There, in place of the stories about the sly trickster Ferdinand of Amezqueta, they had to listen to an old lady tell the story of Theodosius of Goñi, a Navarrese gentleman who, after having killed his father and mother, deceived by the devil, went off to do penance in the hills with a chain on his foot until, after many years had passed and Theodosius was an old man, a dragon approached him and was about to devour him when the archangel St. Michael appeared, killed the dragon and broke the gentleman's chains.

Bautista and Martin thought the tales about good Ferdinand of Amezqueta were more entertaining than this silly story about dragons and saints.

They were listening to the commentaries on the life of Theodosius when a blond man came in and, when he saw Martin and Bautista, stopped and stared at them.

"But, you two!"

"You're the one…"

"The same."

It was the foreigner whom they had freed from the clutches of the Priest.

"What are you doing around here?" asked the foreigner.

"We're going to Estella."

"Really?"

"Yes."

"I am too. We'll go together. Do you know the way?"

"No."

"I do. I've already been there once."

"But what are you doing always going around these places?" Martin asked him.

"It's my job," the foreigner told him.

"Well what are you, if I may ask?"

"I'm a journalist. I wrote a very interesting article about that escape we made. I told about you two and that brunette girl. What a brave young woman!, wasn't she?"

"She sure was."

"So if you have no objection we'll go to Estella together."

"Objection? On the contrary. It would be a pleasure, a great pleasure."

And they agreed to go together.

At 7:00 AM, the time when it began to become light, the three left, crossed the Lizarraga tunnel and started the descent toward the plain of Estella. The stranger was riding a little donkey that was almost going faster than the nags Martin and Bautista had. The road ascended the unevenness of the Andia Mountain Range in a winding course.

They went through positions occupied by Carlist battalions. Among the leaders there were many foreigners with resplendent, rather flamboyant Austrian, Italian and French uniforms.

At mid afternoon they ate in Lezaum and galloping on they passed Abarzuza. On the way the foreigner explained the respective positions of liberals and Carlists in the battle of Monte Muru and told of the place where the fiercest part of the action developed in which General Concha died.

At dusk they were close to Estella.

Long before entering the Carlist court they encountered a company with a lieutenant, who ordered them to stop. The three showed their passports.

When they got close to the Recollect convent it was already night.

"Who goes there?" shouted the sentinel.

"Spain."

"What are you?"

"Spaniards."

"Come ahead."

They again showed their papers to the commander of the guards and entered the Carlist city.

Chapter IX

How Martin and the Foreigner Walked at Night Through Estella and What They Talked About

THEY PASSED THROUGH THE gate of Santiago, went to *Mayor* Street and asked at the inn if there were any rooms available.

A girl appeared on the stairway.

"We're all filled up," she said. "There's no room for three people; only one of you could stay."

"And the horses?" Bautista asked.

"I think there's room in the stable."

The girl went to see about it and Martin said to Bautista:

"Since they only have a place for one person you can stay here. It's best that we separate and pretend we don't know each other."

"Yes, that's true," answered Bautista.

"Tomorrow morning we'll meet in the square."

The girl came back and said that there was room in the stable for the nags.

Bautista stayed there with the animals and the foreigner and Martin left, inquiring at another inn on *Llanos* Street, where they were given rooms.

Martin was taken to a deserted, dusty room at the back of which was a narrow alcove with walls covered with black smoke stains. Obviously the guests killed the bedbugs by burning them with a candle or with the little lamp and left these reassuring traces. The parlor and the alcove smelled like a stable, an odor which came from the joints of the wooden floor.

Martin took out Levi-Alvarez's letter and the package of drafts sewn in the leather of his boot and separated those already accepted and signed from the others. Since all these other drafts were for Estella, he sealed them in an envelope and wrote:

"To the general-in-chief of the Carlist army."

"Would it be wise," he said to himself, "to hand over these drafts without any guarantee whatsoever?"

He did not think about it very long because he realized it would be madness to request a receipt or a guarantee.

"Really, if they don't want to sign I can't make them, and if they give me a receipt and then want to take it away, they can get me in a matter of moments. I'll just have to act indifferent to the whole thing, and if it goes well, take it, and if not, forget it."

He waited for the envelope to dry. He went out to the street and saw a sergeant, and after greeting him, asked:

"Where can I find the general?"

"What general?"

"The general-in-chief. I have some letters for him."

"He's probably out walking in the square. Come on."

They went to the square. Several Carlist generals were walking by the arches in the dull light of some oil street lamps.

The sergeant approached the group and, facing one of them, said, "Sir."

"What is it?"

"This civilian is carrying some letters for the general-in-chief."

Martin came forward and handed him the envelopes. The general leaned against a lamppost and opened them. The general was a tall, thin man, about fifty years old, with a black beard, and he had one arm in a sling. He was wearing a large Gascon cap with a tassel.

"Who brought this?" the general asked in a deep voice.

"I did," replied Martin.

"Did you know what was in here?"

"No, sir."

"Who gave you these envelopes?"

"Mr. Levi-Alvarez, from Bayonne."

"How did you get here?"

"I took a boat from San Juan de Luz to Zumaya; from Zumaya to here I rode a horse."

"And you had no mishap on the way?"

"None."

"There are some papers here that must be given to the king. Do you want to deliver them or do you want me to do it?"

"My only job is to hand over these envelopes and if there is a reply, to take it back to Bayonne."

"Aren't you a Carlist?" asked the general, surprised at Martin's tone of indifference.

"I live in France and I'm a merchant."

"Oh! Well, you're French."

Martin was silent.

"Where are you staying?" the general continued asking.

"At an inn on that street"

"On Llanos street?"

"Yes, I think so. That's the name."

"There's a coach office at the entry, right?"

"Yes, sir."

"Then that's the one. Do you intend to stay in Estella very long?"

"Until I'm told whether there's a reply or not."

"What's your name?"

"Martin Tellagorri."

"Okay. You can go."

Martin bowed and went back to the inn. He met the foreigner at the door.

"Where have you been?" he asked. "I've been looking around for you."

"I went to see the general-in-chief."

"Really?"

"Yes."

"And did you see him?"

"I sure did. And I gave him the letters I brought for him."

"Damn! that's really working fast. I'd hate to have you for a rival on a newspaper. What did he say to you?"

"He was very friendly."

"Be careful, just in case. These fellows are a bunch of crooks."

"I pointed out to him that I'm French."

"Bah! That doesn't matter. This summer they shot a German reporter friend of mine. Be careful."

"Oh! I will."

"Now, let's go have dinner."

They went up the stairs and entered a large kitchen.

Several civilians and soldiers who were gathered there were chatting. They sat down to eat at a long table, illuminated by a brass lamp with several burners which was hanging from the ceiling.

A very short, old man who was presiding over the tables took off his cap and began to pray; all the other diners did likewise, except the foreigner, whom Martin informed of his carelessness, and who, when he realized what was happening, quickly removed his cap.

While they were eating the very short man spoke more than anyone. He was Navarrese, from the shore area. He had a repulsive face, with a pug nose, an oblique look, prominent cheekbones and a small cap tilted over his eyes as if he instinctively wished to conceal them. He was defending the conduct of the killer rebel leader Rosas Samaniego, who was then a prisoner in Estella, and it seemed to him that throwing men down the Igusquiza chasm, if they were liberals and men who blasphemed God and his religion, was a matter of slight importance.

This old man told several stories about the previous Carlist war. One of them was truly odious and cowardly. Once, near a river, going with the band, they met ten or twelve young soldiers who were washing their shirts in the water.

"We bayoneted them all to death," the man said, smiling; then he added hypocritically: "God must have forgiven us."

During the meal the repulsive old man was telling about deeds of this kind. That depraved, vicious character was fanatic, violent and cowardly; he amused himself by telling of his misdeeds; he displayed enough cruelty to conceal his cowardice, enough coarseness to make himself seem frank and enough malice to give himself a clever nature. He had the double stupidity of being a Catholic and a Carlist.

This disagreeable, repugnant individual then began to classify the Carlist battalions according to their merit: first came the Navarrese, as was only natural since he was Navarrese; then the Castilians, followed by the Alavese, then the Guipúzcoans and finally, the Biscayans.

Judging by the course of the conversation it was obvious that there was an atmosphere of strong hatred there: Navarrese, Basques, Alavese, Aragonese, and Castilians had a deadly hatred for one another. All that rather barbaric substance that lies dormant in the provincial Spanish instinct was aroused. They were reproaching each other for being cowards, thugs and thieves.

Martin was feeling very uncomfortable in that den, and leaving his dessert he got up from the table to go. The foreigner followed him and together they went out to the street.

It was drizzling. Groups of soldiers could be seen in some dark taverns in the light of an oil table lamp. The strumming of a guitar was heard; from time to time a voice on the dark, silent street would sing the *jota*.

"That stupid song is really starting to bore me," Martin muttered.

"Which one?" asked the foreigner.

"The jota. I find it rather insolent. It seems like I'm hearing that old Navarrese guy from the inn. The person who sings it means:

> *'I am braver than*
> *anyone, more noble than*
> *anyone, more heroic than*
> *anyone.'"*

"And aren't these Aragonese who sing the jota braver than the other Spaniards?" asked the foreigner, maliciously.

"I don't know; at least I don't believe it. Right now if I had five hundred men I would take Estella by assault and set fire to it."

"Ha, ha! You are an extraordinary man."

"The fact is that I say it because I believe it."

"I believe it too and I regret that you don't have the five hundred men. And what were you saying about the Ebro River people?"

"Nothing; that they themselves have decided that they are the only loyal ones because they talk very roughly and sing the jota."

"So in your opinion this song is like a falsification of valor and strength?"

"Yes, something like that."

"Okay. I'll say that in my next story. Do you dislike my using your opinions?"

"Not at all, because I don't use them for anything."

They continued walking; but when they got a little farther away a sentinel told them to halt and they returned to the square which was deserted.

They walked around for a while and a night watchman greeted them and said:

"What are you doing here?"

"Isn't walking allowed?" Zalacaín asked.

"Sure, man; but this isn't exactly the best time for it."

"Well, we ate dinner late and were taking a stroll," said the foreigner; "we really didn't feel like going to bed so soon."

"Why don't you go there?" said the watchman, pointing to the brightly lighted balcony of a house.

"What's there?" Martin asked.

"The casino," answered the watchman.

"And what are they doing now?" the foreigner questioned.

"They're probably gambling."

They said good night to the watchman and left the square.

Then, taking a turn, they got on Llanos street. A convent bell started to ring.

"Gambling, bells, Carlism and jota. How Spanish all this is, Martin, my friend!" said the foreigner.

"Well, I'm Spanish too and I don't like any of those things," Martin responded.

"Nevertheless, they are the characteristics that make up your country's tradition," said the foreigner.

"The mountains are my country," replied Zalacaín.

Chapter X

What Happened the Second Day in Estella

As previously arranged, Martin and Bautista met in the square. Martin did not think it was a good idea for him to be seen talking to his brother-in-law and to tell him what he had done the night before he wrote down his interview with the general on a piece of paper.

Then he went to the square. The military brass band was playing. There were some soldiers in formation. On the balcony of a small house, opposite the church of St. John, stood Charles with some of his officers.

Martin waited to see Bautista and when he saw him he said:

"Don't let them see us together."

And he handed him the piece of paper.

Bautista went away and shortly afterward he again came up to Martin and gave him another piece of paper.

"I wonder what's going on," Martin said to himself.

He left the square and when he saw that he was alone he read the paper Bautista had given him, which said:

"Be careful. Lefty is here as a sergeant. Don't go around the center of town."

Martin considered Bautista's warning to be of great importance. He knew that Lefty hated him and that being in a position to exercise his authority over him, he could avenge his old grudges with all the passion of that small, violent, irascible man.

Martin crossed the Azucarero bridge, contemplating the greenish water of the river. When he reached the little square where the old town's Mayor Street begins, Martin stopped in front of the palace of the duke of Granada, which had been converted into a jail, to contemplate a fountain with a lion supporter in the middle which held a Navarrese coat of arms in its claws.

He was standing there when he saw the foreigner approaching.

"Hello, Martin, old chum!" he said.

"Hello. Good day."

"Are you going to take a look around this old district?"

"Yes."

"Good, I'll go with you."

They walked along Mayor Street, the main street of the old town. On both sides there were beautiful yellow stone houses with coats of arms and carved figures.

Then, at the end of the road they followed along Tanners street. The old manorial houses displayed their huge, closed entrances; on some of the porches, made into tanner shops, were rows of hanging pelts, and in the background was the greenish, turbid, almost motionless water of the Ega River.

At the end of this street they came upon the church of the Holy Sepulcher and they stopped to look at it. That yellow stone portal with its saints that had had their noses knocked off by people throwing stones at them seemed rather grotesque to Martin, but the foreigner affirmed that it was a magnificent structure.

"Really?" Martin asked.

"Oh, yes indeed!"

"I wonder if the people from around here could have built it," Martin added.

"Do you think it's impossible for the people from Estella to do something well?" asked the foreigner, laughing.

"How should I know? I don't think they've invented gunpowder in this town."

The walls of the old, crumbling, noble houses on a transversal street served as a fence for the gardens. They did not go any farther because there was a patrolman just a short distance away. They came back and went up to St. Peter of the Highroad, a church situated on a hill which could be reached by climbing some worn-down steps with grass growing between the slabs.

"Let's sit down here a while," said the foreigner.

"All right, if you like."

From there they could see all of Estella and the mountains that surround it; below, the roof of the jail and on a hill, the hermitage. An old woman was sweeping the stone steps of the church with a broom, and she was singing very loudly:

> *"Goodbye Plains of Estella,*
> *Saint Benedict and Saint Clara,*
> *Recollect convent,*
> *where I used to walk!"*

"So you see," said the foreigner, "that even though you think so little of this town there are people who are attached to it."

"Who?" asked Martin.

"The person who composed that song."

"It was somebody with bad taste."

The old woman came up to the foreigner and Martin and began a conversation with them. She was a small woman with lively eyes and a tanned complexion.

"You must be a Carlist, eh?" the foreigner asked her.

"Of course. Everyone in Estella is a Carlist, and we're all sure that Charles will make it, with the help of God."

"Yes, that's very likely."

"What do you mean, 'very likely'?" exclaimed the old lady. "It's a sure thing. You must not be from around here."

"No, I'm not a Spaniard."

"Oh, well!"

And the old woman, after looking at him curiously, continued sweeping the steps.

"I think she felt sorry for you when she found out you're not a Spaniard," said Martin.

"Yes, it seems so," replied the foreigner. "The truth is that it's a sad thing for these poor people to be giving up their lives for that stupid, vain man."

"Who do you mean, for Charles?" asked Martin.

"Yes."

"You don't think he's a capable man either?"

"How can he be? He's just an ordinary character without any class. There's nothing original in him. I spoke to him during the bombardment of Irun and you can't imagine anyone duller and more superficial."

"Well, don't say that around here because they'll tear you to pieces. These animals are ready to die for their king."

"Oh! I wouldn't say it. Besides, what good would it do? I couldn't convince anyone; they're either fanatics or adventurers and no one is about to let himself be persuaded. But don't think that they all have great respect either for Charles or for his generals. Haven't you heard them at the inn talking sometimes about Sir Fool? Well, they're referring to the Pretender."

The foreigner and Martin saw the other churches in the town, the Rock and the Castles and the Holy Mary parish and then they went back to eat.

Fortunately, the repugnant little old man was not at the table; however, there was a French legitimist, the Count of Haussonville, from the foreign embassy and a young Carlist officer named Iceta.

The Count of Haussonville was the delight of the table. The count, about forty years old, tall, heavy, straight, blond, was speaking a comical Spanish.

The really funny thing about Haussonville was his voracious appetite. Everything they gave him to eat was only an appetizer for him. He had come from Caspe with a Carlist brigadier general from Valencia as his prisoner, and he was to bring him before Charles' chiefs-of-staff, and he was telling of his expedition in such a way that he made everyone howl with laughter.

He explained his stay in a certain town, with the battalion camped in a church without being able to move on because the snow had made the roads impassable, eating only beans and having a confessional as a toilet, and he gave such details that everyone burst out laughing.

"One day, especially, they brought us some cider," said the Frenchman, "and between the cider and the beans we got so bloated that we had to form a line in front of the confessional. Seldom has such a congregation of the faithful suffering such anxiety to enter the confessional been seen as it was with us. Officers and privates—all of us—were going to the priest's little toilet with heavy hearts to sing our song of the beans."

After cursing the vegetarian diet and the "starchy" diet, he spoke of the rest of his trip.

Each town on the road seemed like a station of the cross for his empty stomach; he remembered the towns by what he had eaten in them, or rather, by what he had gone without; in this town he had been given cabbage broth as a complete meal; in that town a luncheon of boiled greens as a dinner; and to top everything off, he was staying in Estella at the house of some old maids, and in the morning they gave him cocoa with water, in the afternoon, stew and at night, some obnoxious garlic soup.

"And never, never enough," said Haussonville, raising his arms toward the sky.

Iceta was an adventurer. At the beginning he had gotten involved in the war; then he went off to a South American country, took part in a revolution, was later expelled for being a rebel, returned to the Carlist army in which he was already acting impulsively and wanted to get away.

Following him everywhere, as a friend and adviser, was an old servant of his named Asencio, but who was known by these two nicknames: Asenchio Lapurra (Asencio the Thief) and Asenchio Araguiarrapatzallia (Asencio the meat confiscator).

Asencio owed this nickname to the fact that he had been a tax collector in his town.

Asencio was extremely amusing when he spoke Spanish—there was not a single word that he used properly.

Whenever he had to say *gone* he would say *went;* also, he would use *came* for *come* and *don't* for *doesn't.*

The conversation between the Count of Haussonville and Asenchio Lapurra was really peculiar and colorful.

"If they had a good *gen'ral* here," Haussonville would say, "the *wur* would be over."

"It *mayt* be true," Asencio would reply.

"They don't know how to *hendle* a big *urmy*, friend Asencio."

"If they *knowed* anything about *tatics* it would be a different story."

Martin and the foreigner became friendly with Haussonville, Iceta and Asenchio Lapurra, and they laughed loudly at the innumerable *quid pro quos* that were used in the conversation between the Frenchman and the Basque.

Asencio had been in Cuba a while, as a soldier, and he told some anecdotes about that country. What he liked most was to talk about the Chinese.

"They've got the *worstest* intentions but they're good cooks, it's true. *Ast* a Chinaman to make you a mess of rice. He'll make you a *matterpiece*. They're the *queeriest* people. Then they start to say *chop, chop*. And understanding them?—no way. For us?—they only *showt* anger. And whoever they *catched* they *torctured*. Pshaw! We *killt* some of them too."

Martin burst out laughing at the explanations of Asenchio Lapurra.

After eating at the inn Martin, the foreigner, Iceta, Haussonville and Asencio went to a cafe on the square where they talked. There was a religious service at St. John's Church and a number of the pious and some Carlist officers were going there.

"What a country!" said Haussonville; "all people do is go to church. Everything is for the priest: good food, good women… There's nothing you can do here; everything for the priest."

Iceta and Haussonville scornfully watched that mob of people going to church.

"Animals!" exclaimed Iceta, striking the table with his fist. "I'd only like to be able to shoot them."

"Spain! Spain! *Jamais de la vie!* (Never in my life!) A lot of nobility, a lot of masses, a lot of jotas, but not much food."

"War," added Asencio, getting into the conversation, "ain't no good thing."

Chapter XI

How Events Became Involved to the Point thatMartin Slept in Jail His Third Day in Estella

THE NEXT NIGHT MARTIN was getting ready to go to bed when the innkeeper's wife called him and handed him a letter that read:

> *Come tomorrow, at dawn, to the Puy hermitage where*
> *the signed drafts will be returned to you.*
> *—The general-in-chief*

Below there was an illegible signature.

Martin put the letter in his pocket, and seeing that the innkeeper's wife was not leaving his room, he asked:

"Did you want something?"

"Yes; we have been brought two wounded soldiers and we'd like to put one of them in your room. If you'd have no objection, we could move you downstairs."

"Sure; I have no objection."

He went down to a room on the ground floor which was a very big room with two alcoves. In the middle of the room was an altar, illuminated by a few dim oil lamps. Martin went to bed; from his bed he could see quivering lights, but they had no effect on him because he went straight to sleep.

It was past midnight when he awoke somewhat startled. Moans were coming from the adjacent bedroom alternating with cries of "Oh, my God! Oh, my God!"

"What the hell can this be?" thought Martin.

He looked at the clock. It was three A.M. He got back into bed but he could not sleep because of the moaning and thought it would be better to get up. He dressed and went to the adjacent bedroom, opened the curtains and took a look. He could vaguely make out a man lying in the bed.

"What's wrong with you?" asked Martin.

"I'm wounded," muttered the patient.

"Can I get you something?"

"Water."

Martin thought he recognized that voice. He looked around the room for a pitcher of water, and since there was none in the room he went to the kitchen. At the sound of his footsteps, the voice of the landlady asked:

"What's going on?"

"The wounded man wants some water."

"I'm coming."

The landlady appeared in her slip, and handing Martin a little lamp, said:

"Light the way."

They got the water and returned to the room. When he entered the bedroom Martin raised his arm with the lamp in his hand thereby illuminating the patient's face as well as his own. The wounded man took the glass in his hand, and sitting up and looking at Martin, began to shout:

"You? Scum! Thief! Seize him! Seize him!"

The wounded man was Charles Ohando.

Martin set the little lamp on the night table.

"Go away," said the landlady. "He's delirious."

Martin knew that he was not delirious; he withdrew to the parlor and listened to hear whether Charles would tell the landlady anything. Martin waited in his bedroom. In the parlor, under the altar, was Ohando's baggage, consisting of a trunk and a suitcase. Martin thought that perhaps Charles had a letter from Catherine and he said to himself:

"If I get a chance tonight, I'll unlock the trunk."

He never got the chance. It was almost four in the morning when Martin, wrapped in his overcoat, left for the Puy hermitage. The Carlists were engaged in maneuvers. He reached the camp of the pretender Charles and showing his letter, he was allowed to enter.

"His Highness is with two reverend fathers," an officer informed him.

"To hell with His Highness and the reverend fathers," grumbled Zalacaín. "The truth is that this king is ridiculous."

Martin waited for Charles to finish his business with the priests until finally the pompous Bourbon, with his appearance of being well fed, came out of the hermitage, surrounded by his staff. Next to the Pretender was a woman on horseback, whom Martin assumed to be Blanca.

"There's the king. You must kneel and kiss his hand," said the officer.

Zalacaín did not reply.

"And call him 'Your Majesty'"

Zalacaín paid no attention.

Charles took no notice of Martin, and the latter approached the general who handed him the signed drafts. Zalacaín examined them. They were in order.

At that moment a chaplain, displaying wild gestures, began to harangue the troops.

Martin, without anyone noticing, was gradually moving away from there and ran back down to the village. Carrying his fortune in his pocket made him feel more frightened than a rabbit.

At the time when the soldiers went into formation in the square, Martin appeared, and when he saw Bautista he said:

"Go to the church and we'll talk there."

They both entered the church and in a dark chapel they sat down on a bench.

"Take the drafts," Martin told Bautista. "Put them away!"

"Did you get them signed?"

"Yes. We've got to get ready to leave Estella right away."

"I don't know if we can," said Bautista.

"We're in danger here. Besides Lefty, Charles Ohando is in Estella."

"How do you know?"

"Because I've seen him."

"Where?"

"Where I'm staying; he's wounded."

"And did he see you?"

"Yes."

"Sure, they're both here," exclaimed Bautista.

"Both? What do you mean by that?"

"Me? Nothing."

"Do you know something?"

"No, man, no."

"Either you tell me or I'll ask Charles Ohando himself. Is Catherine here?"

"Yes, she's here."

"Really?"

"Yes."

"Where?"

"At the Recollect convent."

"Locked up! And how do you know?"

"Because I've seen her."

"What luck! You've seen her?"

"Yes, I've seen her and talked to her."

"And you wanted to keep it from me! You're no friend of mine, Bautista."

Bautista protested.

"And does she know I'm here?"

"Yes, she knows."

"How can I see her?" asked Zalacaín.

"She usually embroiders in the convent, near the window, and in the afternoon she goes out for a walk in the garden."

"Good. I'm going there. If something happens to me I'll tell that foreigner to go let you know. See if you can rent a coach so we can get out of here."

"I'll see about it."

"As soon as you can."

"All right."

"Goodbye."

"Goodbye and take care."

Martin left the church; he went down Mayor Street toward the Recollect convent; he walked up and down for hours without catching a glimpse of Catherine. At dusk he had the good fortune of seeing her as she appeared at a window. Martin raised his hand and his sweetheart, pretending as if she did not know him, withdrew from the window. Martin remained frozen; then Catherine appeared again and threw a ball of yarn almost at Martin's feet. Zalacaín picked it up; there was a note inside that said: "At eight o'clock we can talk a little. Wait by the fence gate." Martin went back to the inn, ate with an exceptional appetite, and at exactly eight o'clock he was waiting at the fence gate. The Estella church clocks were striking eight when Martin heard two light taps on the gate; he answered in the same way.

"Is it you, Martin?" asked Catherine in a whisper.

"Yes, it is. Can't we see each other?"

"Impossible."

"I'm going to leave Estella. Want to come with me?" asked Martin.

"Yes. But how can I get out of here?"

"Are you willing to do everything I tell you?"

"Yes."

"To follow me everywhere?"

"Everywhere."

"Really?"

"Though it be to die. Now go. For God's sake. Don't let them catch us by surprise."

Martin had forgotten all his danger; he went back and, without thinking about spies, entered the inn to see Bautista and hugged him enthusiastically.

"The day after tomorrow," said Bautista, "we'll have the coach."

"Have you made all the arrangements?"

"Yes."

Martin left his brother-in-law's place gaily whistling. When he came near his inn, two night watchmen, who seemed to be spying on him, approached him and roughly ordered him to keep quiet.

"Man! Can't a person whistle?" asked Martin.

"No, sir."

"Okay. I won't whistle."

"And if you talk back, you'll go to jail."

"I won't talk back."

"Get! Get! To jail."

Zalacaín realized that they were just looking for a pretext to lock him up, and he endured their shoves and between the two night watchmen he entered the jail.

Chapter XII

In Which Events Proceed Rapidly

THE NIGHT WATCHMEN HANDED Martin over to the jailer who took him to a dark room with a bench and a small water pitcher.

"Hell!" exclaimed Martin; "it's very cold in here. Where do I sleep?"

"There's a bench over there."

"Couldn't I get a straw bed and a blanket?"

"If you pay."

"I'll pay whatever it costs. Get me a straw bed and two blankets."

The jailer went off, leaving Martin in the dark, and he returned shortly afterward with a straw bed and the blankets as requested. Martin gave him a dollar, and the jailer, satisfied, asked him:

"What did you do to get here?"

"Nothing. I was just casually walking down the street whistling. And the night watchman said: 'No whistling.' I kept quiet and without further ado they brought me to jail."

"You didn't resist?"

"No."

"Then they must have locked you up for some other reason."

Martin said that he had figured it that way too. The jailer said good night to him; Zalacaín replied pleasantly and stretched out on the floor.

"I am just as safe here as at the inn," he said to himself. "They have me in their hands there as well as here; so it's all really the same. Let's sleep. We'll see what happens tomorrow."

In spite of the fact that his imagination was rebelling against him, he managed to fall deeply asleep.

When he awoke he saw that a beam of sunlight was filtering through a high window, illuminating the poorly furnished, small, dirty room. He knocked on the door, the jailer came, and he asked him:

"Haven't they told you why I'm here?"

"No."

"So they're going to keep me locked up for no reason?"

"Maybe there's been a mistake."

"Well that's a consolation."

"That's life! Nothing can happen to you here."

"You think it's any small matter to be in jail?"

"It's nothing to be ashamed of."

Martin pretended to be the frightened and timid type and asked:

"Will you bring me something to eat?"

"Yeah. You're hungry, eh?"

"I sure am."

"Would you like some mess?"

"No."

"Well, they'll bring you your meal right away."

And the jailer left, gaily singing.

Martin ate what they brought him, stretched out wrapped in the blanket, and after taking a short nap, he got up to make a decision.

"What can I do?" he said to himself. "Bribing the jailer would require a lot of money. If I got word to Bautista I could get him into trouble. If I wait here for them to let me out I could be here the rest of my life; at least I could be a prisoner until the war ends… The only thing I can do is break out."

With this firm decision he began to conceive an escape plan. Getting out through the door was difficult. The door, besides being strong, was closed from the outside with a lock and bolt. Then, even if he got the chance and was able to get out of there, he still had to go down a long corridor and then some stairs… Impossible.

He had to escape through the window. It was the only way.

"Where can this lead to?" he said to himself.

He moved the bench against the wall, got on it, grabbed hold of the thick iron bars and pulled himself up until he was able to look through the grating. The little window faced the square with the fountain where he had met the foreigner the day before.

He jumped to the floor and sat down on the bench. The grating was high and small with three iron bars and no crossbar.

"Pulling one out, perhaps I could get through," Martin said to himself. "And it wouldn't be difficult... But I'd need a rope. Where would I get a rope?... The blanket... I could use the blanket, cut into strips..."

The only tool he had was a small penknife.

"I'll have to see how strong the grating is," he muttered.

He climbed up again. The grating was embedded in the wall, but not too firmly.

The iron bars were held by a wooden frame, and the frame, at one end, was rotted. Martin imagined that it would not be difficult to cut into the wood and remove the iron bar on one side.

He cut a strip from the blanket, and passing it around the middle bar and then tying it at the ends, he formed a hoop-clasp into which he placed two of the bench legs and the other two he set on the floor.

Thus he had a kind of inclined plane on which to reach the grating. He slid his way up, grabbed a bar with his left hand, and with his right hand holding the penknife, he began to chip away the wood of the frame.

The position was not at all comfortable, but Zalacaín's determination did not weaken, and after an hour of hard work he succeeded in wrenching the iron bar from its hole.

When he had it loose he put it back again as it was before; he replaced the bench on the floor, hid the splinters he had cut from the window frame in his straw bed and waited for night to come.

The jailer brought him his dinner and Martin eagerly asked whether anything had been decided about his case, whether they were intending to keep him imprisoned without any reason whatsoever.

The jailer shrugged his shoulders and withdrew immediately, humming a tune.

Just as soon as Zalacaín was alone he went to work.

He was absolutely positive that he could escape. He took out his penknife and began to cut the two blankets from top to bottom. Once this was done he started tying the strips together until he had a rope, some ninety feet in length, which was what he needed.

Then he thought he would leave a happy, amusing remembrance in the cell. He took the little water pitcher, put his cap over it and placed it in the straw bed wrapped in the piece of blanket that was left.

"When the jailer peeps in he'll think I'm still sleeping. If I gain a couple hours with this, it will really help me to get away."

He contemplated the bulge with a smile; then he climbed up to the grating, tied one end of the rope to the two iron bars and dropped the other end outside little by little. When the entire rope was hanging along the wall, he laboriously squeezed through the opening left by the missing bar and began to slide down against the wall.

He passed right by a lighted window through which he saw someone moving. He was about four or five yards above the street when he heard the sound of footsteps. He stopped his descent and the footsteps were beginning to fade away when he dropped to the ground with a thud.

One of the knots must have come loose because he had a piece of rope in his hand. He got up.

"No harm done. I'm all right," he said to himself.

As he passed by the fountain in the square he threw the rest of the rope in the water. Then he hurriedly went along Rua Street.

He was moving onward, turning around to look back, when in the light of a quivering lantern hanging from a rope he saw two men carrying rifles with sinisterly glistening bayonets. These men obviously were following him. If he kept going much farther he would run across the guard stationed outside the walls. Not knowing what to do and seeing an open vestibule door, he entered, and gently pushing the door, closed it.

He heard the sound of the men's footsteps on the sidewalk. He waited for them to go away and when he was about to leave, an old woman came down to the vestibule and locked and bolted the door.

Martin was locked in the house. The footsteps of the pursuers were heard again.

"They're still out there," he thought.

In fact, not only were they still out there but they pounded twice on the door with the large knocker.

The old woman appeared again with a lantern and began talking to the men outside without opening the door.

"Has any man come in here?" asked one of the pursuers.

"No."

"Will you check to make sure? We're from the night patrol."

"There's nobody here."

"Look around the vestibule."

Martin, when he heard this, concealing himself, left the vestibule and reached the stairway. The old woman shined the lantern light all around the vestibule and said:

"There's no one, no; there's no one here."

Martin tried to return to the vestibule but the old woman placed the lantern in such a way that it lighted the bottom of the stairway. The only thing Martin could do was go back up and climb the stairs two at a time.

"We'll spend the night here," he said to himself.

There was no exit whatsoever. The best thing was to wait for daylight and for the door to be opened. He did not want to take the risk of being found inside with the house locked, and he waited until rather late in the morning.

It was probably about nine o'clock when he began to go cautiously down the stairs. As he was passing by the second floor he saw a Carlist officer's uniform, complete with cap and sword, laid out on a sofa in a very luxurious room. Martin was so convinced that only through boldness could he save himself that he quickly took off his clothes, put on the uniform and cap, strapped on the sword, wrapped himself in his coat and began to walk on his heels down the stairs. He met the old woman from the night before, and when he saw her he said:

"But isn't there anyone in this house?"

"What did you want? I hadn't seen you."

"Does Major Charles Ohando live here?"

"No, sir; he doesn't live here."

"Thank you!"

Martin went out to the street and, disguised and with a martial attitude, he went to the inn where Bautista was staying. "You!" exclaimed

Urbide. "Where did you get that uniform? What were you doing all day yesterday? I was worried. What's happening?"

"I'll tell you everything. Do you have the coach?"

"Yes, but..."

"There's no time; bring it right away, as soon as you can. But fast."

Martin sat down at the table and wrote in pencil on a piece of paper:

Dear sister. I have to see you. I am seriously wounded. Come immediately with my friend Zalacaín in the coach.

Your brother, Charles.

After writing the note Martin paced the floor impatiently. Each minute seemed like a century to him. He had to stay there waiting in mortal anguish for two very long hours. Finally, around twelve o'clock, he heard the sound of small bells.

He went to the balcony to take a look. At the door waited a coach pulled by four horses. Among them Martin recognized the two nags they had ridden from Zumaya to Estella. The coach, an old, rickety landau, had a window and one of the lanterns tied with a rope.

Martin came down the stairs wrapped in his cloak, opened the coach door and said to Bautista:

"To the Recollect convent."

Bautista, making no reply, headed for the place indicated. When the coach stopped in front of the convent, Bautista, when Zalacaín got out, said:

"What mad scheme do you have now? Look before you leap."

"Do you know the way to Logroño?" asked Martin.

"Yes."

"Then take it."

"But..."

"Just do as I say; take it. At first go slowly so you don't wear out the horses, but then you'll have to race."

Having given this advice, Martin, very erect, went toward the convent.

"We're really going to have a fine time," Bautista said to himself, getting ready for the catastrophe.

Martin knocked, entered the vestibule, asked the doorkeeper nun for Miss Ohando and told her that he had to give her a letter. He was taken to the locutory and there he met Catherine and a fat nun who was the mother superior. He greeted them profoundly and asked:

"Miss Ohando?"

"Yes, I am."

"I have a letter for you from your brother."

Catherine grew pale and her hands trembled with emotion. The mother superior, a big woman with an ivory color, big, dark eyes like two black spots that covered half her face, and several moles on her chin, asked:

"What is it? What does the note say?"

"It says that my brother is seriously ill…, that I should come," stuttered Catherine.

"Is he that bad?" the mother superior asked Martin.

"Yes, I believe so."

"Where is he?"

"At a house on the Logroño road," replied Martin.

"Toward Azqueta, perhaps?"

"Yes, near Azqueta. He was wounded on a reconnaissance mission."

"Okay. We'll go," said the mother superior.

"Have Benedict, the messenger, come too."

Martin did not object and waited for them to get ready to escort them. When the four came out to the coach and when Bautista saw them from the coachbox, he could not help but grimace with astonishment. The messenger climbed up and sat next to him.

"Let's go," Martin said to Bautista.

The coach started off; the mother superior closed the curtains and, taking out a rosary, began to pray. The coach went down Mayor Street, crossed the Azucarero bridge, St. Nicholas street, and got on the Logroño road.

When they got out of the town a Carlist patrol stopped the coach.

Someone opened the door and closed it again right away.

"The mother superior from the Recollect convent is going to visit a patient," said the messenger in a twangy voice.

The coach continued on, at the slow trot of the horses. It was drizzling, the night was dark, not a single star was shining in the sky. They passed a village, then another.

"How slowly we're going!" exclaimed the nun.

"That's because the horses aren't any good," replied Martin.

They quickly passed another village and when there were no towns nor houses ahead or behind in sight, Bautista lessened the pace. It was growing darker.

"But what's happening?" asked the mother superior suddenly. "Aren't we there yet?"

"What's happening, ma'am," answered Zalacaín, "is that we must keep going."

"And why?"

"That's the order."

"And who has given that order?"

"I can't tell you."

"Well, please stop the coach because I'm going to get out."

"If you want to get out alone, you may do so."

"No, I'll go with Catherine."

"Impossible."

The mother superior cast an angry glance at Catherine and when she saw that the girl was lowering her eyes, she exclaimed:

"Oh! The two of you were in on this together."

"Yes, we are in on this together," answered Martin. "This girl is my fiancée and she doesn't want to stay at the convent; she wants to marry me."

"That's a lie; I'll prevent it."

"You won't prevent it because you won't be able to prevent it."

The mother superior kept quiet. The coach continued its tedious, monotonous pace along the road. It was already midnight when they came into view of Los Arcos.

Bautista stopped the horses a few hundred yards before reaching it and jumped down from the coachbox.

"You," he said to Zalacaín in Basque, "We have a footworn horse; if you could change it here…"

"We'll try."

"If the two of them could be changed, it would be better."

"I'll go see. Watch the messenger and the nun; don't let them get away."

Martin unharnessed the horses and took them to the inn.

A chubby, very pretty girl in a very bad mood appeared. Martin told her what he needed and she replied that it was impossible, that the boss was in bed.

"Well, we'll have to wake him up."

They called the innkeeper, who presented a number of obstacles; he gave all kinds of excuses, but when he saw Martin's uniform he agreed to obey and ordered that the porter be awakened. The porter was not there.

"You see, the porter isn't in."

"Help me and don't get upset," Martin said to the girl, taking her hand and giving her a dollar. "My life is at stake."

The girl put the money in her apron and she herself brought out two horses from the stable and led them, gaily singing:

> *The Puy Virgin from Estella*
> *said to the one from Pilar:*
> *If you are Aragonese,*
> *I am Navarrese and saltier by far.*

Martin paid the innkeeper and reached an agreement with him concerning the place where he was to leave the horses in Logroño.

Bautista, Martin and the girl, working together, completely replaced the team. Martin escorted the girl and when she was safely back home he squeezed her by the waist and kissed her on the cheek.

"You're a dimwit too!" she exclaimed impudently.

"Well, you're Navarrese and salty and I want to taste that salt," replied Martin.

"Just be careful it doesn't hurt you. Who are you taking in the coach?"

"Some old ladies."

"Will you be coming back this way?"

"As soon as I can."

"Well, goodbye."

"Goodbye, beautiful. Listen, if you're asked which way we went, tell them we stayed here."

"Okay, I'll do it."

The coach passed by Los Arcos. As it was approaching Sansol, four men blocked the road.

"Halt!" shouted one of them who was holding a lantern.

Martin jumped from the coach and drew his sword.

"Who are you?" he asked.

"Royalist volunteers," they said.

"What do you want?"

"To see if you have passports."

Martin took out his passport and showed it. An old man with a respectable appearance took the paper and began to read it.

"Can't you see I'm an officer?" asked Martin.

"It doesn't matter," replied the old man. "Who's inside?"

"Two Recollect nuns going to Logroño."

"Don't you people know the liberals are in Viana?" asked the old man.

"That's all right. We'll get by."

"Let's take a look at those ladies," muttered the ridiculous old man.

"Hey, Bautista! Be careful," Martin said in Basque.

Urbide got down from the coachbox and the messenger jumped behind him. The old patrol leader opened the coach door and shined the lantern light on the faces of the lady travelers.

"Who are you men?" asked the mother superior hastily.

"We are volunteers of Charles VII."

"Then keep us here. These men are kidnapping us."

She had scarcely finished saying this when Martin kicked the lantern that the old man was holding; then with a shove he threw the respectable old man into the ditch at the side of the road. Bautista grabbed the rifle from another one of the night patrolmen, and the messenger was being attacked by two men at the same time.

"But I'm not with these fellows! I'm a Carlist," shouted the messenger.

The men, convinced, assaulted Zalacaín, who fought with both of them; one of the volunteers stabbed him with his bayonet in the left shoulder and Martin, enraged with the pain, thrust his sword straight through the man's body.

The patrol had decided to flee, leaving a rifle on the ground.

"Are you wounded?" Bautista asked his brother-in-law.

"Yes, but I don't think it's serious. Come on, let's go!"

"Shall we take this rifle?"

"Yes. Take the cartridge pouch from that one I stabbed and let's get moving."

Bautista handed Martin a rifle and a pistol.

"Let's go. Inside!" Martin said to the messenger, who got in the coach trembling. The horses pulled them away at a gallop. They passed through the center of a town. Some windows were opened and the residents came out, obviously thinking that a caisson was passing through the town. A half hour later Bautista stopped the coach. A leather strap had broken and they had to fix it by making a hole with the penknife. It was raining very hard and the road was becoming muddy.

"We'll have to go slower," said Martin.

And in fact they began to slow the pace, but fifteen minutes later a sound which seemed to be the galloping of horses was heard in the distance. Martin looked out the window; undoubtedly they were being chased.

The sound of the hoofbeats was getting closer and closer.

"Halt! Halt!" they shouted.

Bautista whipped the horses and the coach moved at a dizzying speed. When it took the turns the old landau would bend and creak as if it were going to break into pieces. The mother superior and Catherine were praying; the messenger was groaning in the back of the coach.

"Halt! Halt!" they shouted again.

"Go on, Bautista! Go on!" said Martin, sticking his head out the little window.

At that moment a shot rang out and a bullet went whizzing past, just missing them. Martin loaded the pistol, saw a horse and rider approaching the coach, fired and the horse fell to the ground with a thud. The pursuers shot at the coach which was pierced with bullets. Then Martin loaded the rifle, and squeezing his body through the little window, he began to shoot in the direction of the sound of the hoofbeats. The pursuers were firing too but the night was dark and neither Martin nor the enemy was able to hit the target. Bautista, crouching in the coachbox, was keeping the horses at a gallop; none of the animals was wounded; things were going well.

The chase ended at dawn. There was no longer anyone in sight on the road.

"I think we can stop," shouted Bautista. "Don't you? We've got a broken strap again. Do we stop?"

"Yeah, stop," said Martin; "there's no one around."

Bautista stopped and they again had to repair another leather strap.

The messenger was praying and groaning inside the coach; Zalacaín had to use force to get him out.

"Come on, up to the coachbox," he told him. "Don't you have any blood in your veins, you damned sacristan?" he asked.

"I'm a peaceful man and I don't like getting mixed up in these things and I don't like hurting anybody," he replied snarling.

"I wonder if you're a nun in disguise."

"No, I'm a man."

"Can you possibly have been mistaken?"

"No, I'm a man, a humble man, if you like."

"That won't prevent you from getting some lead pellets in that cold fat you call a body."

"How ghastly!"

"Therefore, you must understand, lazy, that when one is faced with either killing or getting killed, one cannot fool around or just pray."

Martin's harsh words aroused the messenger somewhat.

As Bautista was climbing up to the coachbox, Martin said to him: "Do you want me to take over now?"

"No, no. I'm all right. And you, how's your wound?"

"Nothing serious."

"Let's have a look at it."

"Later, later; we can't lose any more time."

Martin opened the coach door and when he sat down, addressing the mother superior, he said: "As for you, ma'am, if you scream again I'll tie you to a tree and leave you along the road."

Catherine, extremely frightened, was crying. Bautista went up to the coachbox and the messenger with him. The coach started off slowly, but not long afterward the sound of hoofbeats was heard again.

They no longer had any ammunition left and the horses were tired.

"Let's go, Bautista; give it all you've got," shouted Martin, with his head out the little window. "That's it! Get hot."

Bautista, excited, was shouting and cracking the whip. The coach was moving at an amazing speed, and soon the sound of hoofbeats behind faded away.

Dawn was now starting to break; large gray clouds were being blown around by the wind, and in the background of the gloomy, reddish dawn sky a town on a hill could be discerned. It was probably Viana.

As they were approaching it, the coach struck a rock, one of the wheels came off, the wagon tipped over and hit the ground. All the travelers were turned upside down and fell in the mud. Martin got up first and took Catherine in his arms.

"Are you all right?" he asked her.

"Yes; I think so," she answered, groaning.

The mother superior had received a bump on the forehead and the messenger a disjointed wrist.

"There aren't any serious injuries," said Martin. "Let's get moving!"

The travelers sang a chorus of complaints and moans.

"We'll unharness and ride horseback," said Bautista.

"Not me. I'm not moving from here," responded the mother superior.

The arrival of the coach and its disastrous fall had not gone unnoticed because a few minutes later half a company of soldiers came forward from Viana.

"It's the liberal rural police," Bautista said to Martin.

"That's good."

The half company approached the group.

"Halt!" shouted the sergeant. "Who goes there?"

"Spain."

"Surrender."

"Take us."

The sergeant and his troops were amazed when they saw a Carlist soldier, two nuns and their companions covered with mud.

"Let's go to town," they ordered them.

All of them together, escorted by the soldiers, arrived in Viana.

A lieutenant who came along the road asked:

"What's up, sergeant?"

"We've captured a Carlist general and two nuns." Martin wondered why the sergeant was calling him a Carlist general; but when he saw that the lieutenant was saluting him, he realized that the uniform he had picked up in Estella belonged to a general.

Chapter XIII

How They Arrived in Logroño and What Happened to Them

THEY MADE THEM ALL enter a guard barracks where several soldiers were sleeping on old cots and others were warming up by the heat of a big fireplace. Martin was treated with a great deal of respect because of his uniform. He requested that the officer allow Catherine to stay at his side.

"Is she your wife?"

"Yes, she is."

The officer granted the request and led them both to a shabby room which was being used by officers.

The mother superior, Bautista, and the messenger were not worthy of such attention and they remained in the small barracks.

An old Andalusian sergeant fell in love with the mother superior and began to flatter her with classical remarks: he told her that her *eyeth were like two thtarth* and that she looked like the Virgin of the *Contholathion* of Utrera, and he added a number of other things from the almanac repertory.

Bautista thought that the Andalusian's compliments were so funny that he had a difficult time restraining his laughter.

"You better *thut* up, you dirty *Carlitht,*" the sergeant told him.

"I didn't say a word," replied Bautista.

"If you don't *thtop* laughing like that I'm going to *thtick* you like a toad."

Bautista had to go off to a corner to laugh, and the mother superior and the sergeant continued their conversation.

A colonel, who gave Martin a military salute when he saw him, arrived at noon. Martin told him of his adventures but the colonel frowned when he heard them.

"These soldiers," thought Martin, "don't like it when a civilian does something more difficult than they've done."

"You people will go to Logroño and there we'll see if we can find out who you are. What's wrong? Are you wounded?"

"Yes."

"I'll send the doctor to examine you."

In fact, a doctor came to examine Martin, bandaged him and fixed the dislocated wrist of the messenger who shouted and shrieked like a condemned man. After eating they brought the horses from the coach, made them mount, and guarded by the entire company, they took the Logroño road.

When they got close to the bridge over the Ebro River, a number of washwomen and wives of carabineers came out to see the strange procession, and several of them began to sing, especially to the nun:

> *Now you must really be very happy,*
> *You yellow Carlist female;*
> *now you must really be very happy,*
> *you big, yellow Carlist.*

The poor mother superior was livid with rage. Martin and Bautista were looking at each other in a kind of comical amazement.

In Logroño they stopped at a barracks and an officer had Martin go up to see the general. Zalacaín related his adventures and the general said:

"If I were certain that what you are telling me is true, I would set you and your companions free immediately."

"And how can I prove that what I've told you is the truth?"

"If you could only prove your identity! Don't you know anyone here? Some merchant?"

"No."

"Too bad."

"Oh, yes; I do know somebody," Martin stated suddenly; "I know Mrs. Briones and her daughter."

"And Captain Briones, I suppose you know him too?"

"Right."

"Well, I'll call him; he'll be here in a few minutes."

The general sent an aide of his and a half hour later Captain Briones arrived and identified Martin. The general set them all free.

Martin, Catherine and Bautista were about to leave together, despite the opposition of the mother superior, when Captain Briones said:

"Friend Zalacaín, my mother and sister demand that you have dinner with them."

Martin explained to his fiancée how it would be impossible for him to disregard the invitation, and leaving Bautista and Catherine, he left with the officer.

Mrs. Briones' house was on a centrally located street that had porticos.

Rosie and her mother gave Martin a very warm reception. The adventure of his arrival in Logroño with a young lady and a nun had spread all over town.

They both asked him one question after another and Martin had to relate his adventures.

"But, what a fellow!" Josephine was saying, making the sign of the cross. "You're a real devil."

After dinner some girl friends of Rose Briones came and Martin had to recount his adventures one more time. Then they had an after-dinner chat and sang. Martin was thinking: "I wonder what Catherine is doing." But then he forgot about her during the conversation.

Josephine said that her daughter had gotten the whim to learn to play the guitar, and she urged her to sing.

"Yes, sing," said the other girls.

"Yes, please do," added Zalacaín.

Rosie took out her guitar and sang some songs, accompanying herself and then, in honor of Martin's visit, she sang a zortzico in Spanish that began like this:

Although the Angelus may sound,
I choose to remain behind;
the girl with the red kerchief,
has made me lose my mind.

And the refrain of the song was:

Get up, for the Angelus
is about to ring, you see.
Get up, for I love you,
darling, darling; come to me.

And when she sang this, Rosie was looking at Martin with her sparkling, dark eyes in such a way that he forgot that Catherine was waiting for him.

When he left Mrs. Briones' house it was nearly eleven o'clock at night. When he reached the street he became aware of his cruel lack of attention. He went looking for his fiancée, inquiring at the hotels. Most of them were closed. At one of them he was told:

"There is a young lady staying here but she's resting in her room."

"Couldn't you tell her I'm here?"

"No."

Bautista could not be found either.

Not knowing what to do, Martin returned to the porticos and began to walk through them. "If it weren't for Catherine," he thought, "I would be able to stay here and find out whether Rosie Briones really cares for me as it seems she does."

He was engrossed in these thoughts when a man who looked like a servant stopped in front of him and said:

"Are you Mr. Martin Zalacaín?"

"I am."

"Will you come with me? My mistress wants to talk to you."

"And who is your mistress?"

"I was told to inform you that she is a childhood friend of yours."

"A childhood friend of mine?"

"Yes."

"It's not possible," thought Zalacaín. "Can I have known someone in my childhood who has servants without realizing it? Well, let's go see my friend," he said aloud.

The servant went on through the porticos, turned a corner, pushed open the door of a big house and entered an elegant vestibule lighted by a large lantern.

"Come in, sir," said the servant, pointing out a carpeted stairway.

"This must be a mistake," thought Martin. "What else could it be?"

They went up the stairway; the servant raised a curtain and Zalacaín entered. Sitting on a sofa leafing through an album was an unknown woman, a small, slender, blonde, very elegant woman.

"Excuse me, ma'am," said Martin, "I think we're both the victims of a mistake."

"I, at least, am not," she answered, laughing waggishly.

"Would you like anything else, ma'am?" asked the servant.

"No, you may leave."

Martin was astonished. The servant drew the heavy curtain and the two of them remained alone.

"Martin," said the lady, getting up from her seat and putting her small hands on his shoulders. "Don't you remember me?"

"No, not really."

"I'm Linda."

"Linda who?"

"Linda, the one who was in Urbia with the tamer when your mother died. Don't you remember?"

"You, ma'am, are Linda?"

"Oh, don't be so formal! Yes, I'm Linda. I found out about your arrival in Logroño and I sent for you."

"So you're that little girl who was playing with the bear?"

"The same."

"And you recognized me?"

"Yes."

"I would not have recognized you."

"Speak, tell me about your life. You don't know how much I wanted to see you. You're the only man for whom I ever got a beating. Remember? To me you were my whole family. What can he be doing? Where can Martin be?—I used to think."

"Really? How strange! It's been such a long time! And we're both still young."

"Tell me! Tell me! What kind of a life have you had? What have you been doing with yourself?"

Martin, excited, spoke of his life and adventures. Then Linda told the story of her Bohemian existence as an acrobat until a rich gentleman took her out of the circus and offered her his protection. Now this man, who had a title and extensive holdings in the Rioja region, wanted to marry her.

"And are you going to get married?" Martin asked her.

"Of course."

"So in a short time you'll be a countess or a marchioness?"

"Yes, a marchioness; but, boy it doesn't thrill me. I have always lived a free life and I just can't be held in chains, even though they're made of gold. But you look pale. What's wrong?"

Martin felt very fatigued and his shoulder was hurting. When she discovered he was wounded, Linda made him stay there.

Fortunately it was only a minor scratch and Zalacaín soon recovered.

The next day Linda did not allow him to leave; and when he saw that he was being dominated by her, by her gentle charm, the patient realized that his convalescence was more dangerous to his feelings than to his health.

"Have somebody tell my brother-in-law where I am," Martin said to Linda several times.

She sent a servant to the hotels, but neither Bautista nor Catherine could be found in any of them.

Chapter XIV

How Zalacaín and Bautista Urbide Single-handedly Captured the City of Laguardia, Occupied by the Carlists

IF MARTIN HAD BEEN acquainted with the *Odyssey*, it is possible that it would have occurred to him to compare Linda to the witch Circe and himself to Ulysses; but since he had not read Homer's poem, he did not think of such a comparison.

It did occur to him several times that he was behaving very rudely. But Linda was so charming! She showed such great enthusiasm for him! She had made him forget Catherine. For many days he cursed his rudeness but yet he stayed. He decided, in his conscience, that Bautista was to blame for everything, and this decision comforted him.

"Where has that man gone?" he was wondering.

A week after his meeting with Linda, as he was walking through the porticos of the main street in Logroño, he met Bautista, who was coming toward him, indifferent and calm as usual.

"Where have you been?" exclaimed Martin, angrily.

"That's what I'd like to know—where have you been?" replied Bautista.

"And Catherine?"

"How do I know! I thought you'd know where she was and that you two had gone away without even telling me."

"So you don't know?"

"Nope."

"When was the last time you talked to her?"

"The same day we got here—a week ago. When you went to have dinner at Mrs. Briones' house, Catherine, the nun, and I went to the inn. It got later and later and you didn't show up.

'But where is he?' Catherine asked. 'How do I know?' I said to her. At one in the morning, seeing that you weren't coming, I went to bed. I was fatigued. I fell asleep and woke up very late and I discovered that the nun and Catherine had left and you had not come. I waited one day, and since no one showed up, I went to Bayonne and left the drafts with Levi-Alvarez. Then your sister began to say to me, 'But where can Martin be? Has something happened to him?' I wrote to Briones and he answered saying that you were here shocking the town, and so I came back."

"Yes, actually I am to blame," said Martin. "Where do you suppose Catherine is? Can she have gone with the nun?"

"That would seem most likely."

Martin, finding himself talking to Bautista, felt that he was beyond the influence of Linda's spell and began very actively making inquiries. The two lady travelers who had stayed at the hotel had both left the same day—one supposedly for the station, and the other in a coach going to Laguardia.

Martin and Bautista imagined that the two women might be taking refuge in Laguardia. Obviously the nun regained her influence over Catherine in Martin's absence and convinced her to return to the convent with her.

The fact that Catherine had not written could not be explained in any other way.

They were determined to follow the nun's trail. They found out at the Asa inn that several days before a coach carrying the nun attempted to get through to Laguardia; but when they saw that the road was being occupied by the liberal army, which was laying siege to the city and attacking the trenches, they retreated. The people at the inn thought that the nun had probably gone back to Logroño, unless she had tried to enter the besieged city, taking the Lanciego road on horseback through Oyon and Venaspre.

They went to Oyon and then to Yecora but nobody could tell them anything. The two towns were almost totally abandoned.

From that high road one could see Laguardia, surrounded by its wall, in the midst of an enormous, open, level space. To the north the Cantabrian Mountain Range bound this open space like a gray wall; to the south one could see as far as the Pancorbo Mountains.

In this yellowish polygon of Laguardia neither roofs nor belfries stood out; it seemed more like a fortress than a town. At one end of the wall there rose a fortified tower, wrapped at that moment in a dense cloud of smoke.

When they left Yecora a hungry-looking man in rags came up to them and spoke. He told them that the Carlists would abandon Laguardia any day now. Martin asked him if it was possible to enter the city.

"Through the gate it's impossible," said the man, "but I've gotten in by climbing up some holes in the wall between the Paganos and Mercadal gates."

"But what about the sentinels?"

"There usually aren't any around."

Martin and Bautista went down along a path from Lanciego to the road and reached the place where the liberal army was camped. The troops, after bombarding the Carlist trenches, were moving forward and the enemy was abandoning their positions, retreating to the walls.

Captain Briones' regiment was at the front. Martin asked for him and found him. Briones introduced Zalacaín and Bautista to some officer friends of his, and at night they played cards and drank. Martin won and one of Briones' friends, an Aragonese lieutenant who had lost his entire salary in the game, in order to get revenge, began to say bad things about the Basques; he and Martin became involved in a stupid argument about regional chauvinism of the kind that is so frequent in Spain.

The Aragonese lieutenant was saying that the Basques were so feeble-minded that a Carlist captain, in order to teach them to march to the right and to the left, would carry a bunch of straw in his hand and would say to them, for example: "Column right!" And he would immediately switch the straw to his right hand and say: "In the direction of the straw!" Besides, according to the officer, the Basques were a bunch of cowards who did not want to fight unless they were close to home.

Martin was becoming irritated and said to the officer:

"I don't know what the Basques may be like, but I can say this—whatever you or any of these gentlemen can do, I can do with ease."

"That goes for me too," said Bautista, joining Martin's side.

"Come on, man," said Briones. "Don't be foolish. Lieutenant Ramirez didn't mean to offend you."

"He only called us stupid and cowards," Martin said laughing. "Of course I really don't care at all what this gentleman thinks about us, but I would like to have a chance to prove to him that he's wrong."

"Step outside," said the lieutenant.

"Whenever you like," replied Martin.

"No," responded Briones, "I forbid it. Lieutenant Ramirez will be arrested."

"All right," grumbled the lieutenant. "If these gentlemen want a little fun, when we take Laguardia they can come with us," the officer remarked.

Martin thought he detected a note of irony in the officer's words and mockingly answered:

"When you guys take Laguardia! No, man. That's nothing for us. I'll go to Laguardia alone and take it, or at the most with my brother-in-law, Bautista."

They all began to laugh at the boast, but seeing that he kept insisting, saying that that very night he was going to enter the besieged city, they thought Martin was crazy. Briones, who knew him, tried to persuade him not to do this rash thing, but Zalacaín would not change his mind.

"Do you men see this white handkerchief?" he said. "Tomorrow, at dawn, you will see it on this stick waving over Laguardia. Is there a rope around here?"

One of the young officers brought a rope and Martin and Bautista, without paying any attention to what Briones was saying, started going down the road.

The cold night air calmed them and Martin and his brother-in-law looked at each other in wonderment. They say that the ancient Goths had the custom of settling their affairs twice—once, drunk and once, sober. In this way they combined boldness and prudence in their decisions. Martin regretted not having followed this wise Gothic method, but he kept quiet and he let it be understood that this was not one of the happiest moments of his life.

"What? Are you going?" asked Bautista.

"We'll try."

They were getting closer to Laguardia. A short distance from its walls they turned to the left, along the *Senda de las Damas,* until they got to the *El Ciego* road, and crossing it they approached the height on which the city is located. They passed by the cemetery and reached a walk with trees that circles the town.

They must have been at the point indicated by the man from Yecora, between the Mercadal and Paganos gates.

As a matter of fact, that was the place. They found the holes in the wall that were used as a stairway; the lower ones were closed up.

"We could open these gaps," said Bautista.

"Hmm! It would take a while," replied Martin. "Get up on my shoulders and see if you can make it. Take the rope."

Bautista climbed up on Martin's shoulders and then, seeing that it was possible to get up without any difficulty, he scaled the wall to the top. He looked over and, not seeing any guards, he jumped.

"No one?" asked Martin.

"No one."

Bautista tied the rope with a slipknot on a corner of a tower and Martin pulled himself up, with the stick between his teeth.

The two men slipped along the edge of the wall until they came to an alley. Not a guard nor a sentinel; nothing could be seen nor heard. The town seemed dead.

"What can be happening here?" Martin said to himself.

They approached the other end of the city. The same silence. No one. Without a doubt the Carlists had fled from Laguardia.

Martin and Bautista became convinced that the town was abandoned. They kept going confidently until they got near the Mercadal gate, and opposite the cemetery, toward the Logroño road, they planted the stick between two rocks and tied the white handkerchief to the top.

Once this was done they quickly returned to the place where they had scaled the wall. The rope was still there where they had left it. Dawn was breaking. From up there one could see a huge expanse of country land. The daylight was beginning to indicate the shadows of the vineyards and olive groves. The cool breeze was announcing the proximity of day.

"Okay, go down," said Martin. "I'll hold the rope."

"No, you go down," replied Bautista.

"Come on, don't be an idiot."

"Who goes there?" shouted a voice at that very moment.

Neither of them answered. Bautista began to go down slowly. Martin stretched out on the wall.

"Who goes there?" the sentinel shouted again.

Martin flattened himself on the ground as much as he could; a shot rang out and a bullet passed over his head. Fortunately, the sentinel was far away. When Bautista had gone down, Martin began to descend. He was lucky that the rope did not slip. Bautista was waiting for him with his heart in his mouth. There was movement on the wall; four or five men appeared on it, and Martin and Bautista hid behind the trees of the walk that surrounded the town. The bad thing was that it was becoming lighter and lighter. They kept moving from tree to tree until they got close to the cemetery.

"All we can do now is make a run for it in the open," said Martin. "One…, two…, three…, go!"

They both started running. Several shots sounded. They reached the cemetery safely. From there they quickly got to the Logroño road. Now that they were out of danger they looked back. The handkerchief was still on the wall waving in the wind. Briones and his friends received Martin and Bautista as heroes.

The next day the Carlists abandoned Laguardia and took refuge in Peñacerrada. The townspeople raised high a flag of truce and the army, with the general at the head, entered the city.

Although Martin and Bautista inquired all over town, they did not find Catherine.

Part III

The Last Adventures

Chapter 1

The Newlyweds Are Happy

CATHERINE WAS NOT INFLEXIBLE. A few days later Martin received a letter from his sister. Ignacia said that Catherine had been at her house in Zaro for several days. At first she had not wanted to hear anything about Martin, but now she was forgiving him and waiting for him.

Martin and Bautista appeared in Zaro immediately, and the sweethearts became reconciled.

Arrangements for the wedding were made. What peace they were enjoying there while people were being killed in Spain! Folks were working in the fields. After mass on Sundays the villagers, wearing their finest, with their jackets over their shoulders, would gather at the cider shop and the pelota court; the women would go to church in their black cloaks with hoods over their heads. Catherine sang in the choir and Martin would go to hear her as he did in his childhood when she used to sing the Hallelujah in the church of Urbia.

The wedding was celebrated with all possible solemnity in the church of Zaro, and then the reception was held at Bautista's house.

It was still cold, and friends from the village gathered in the kitchen of the house which was big, beautiful, and clean. Piles of wood were thrown into the huge, round fireplace, and the guests sang and drank well into the night by the light of the flames. Bautista's parents, who were old and wrinkled and could only speak Basque, sang a monotonous song from their day, and Bautista exhibited his voice and his complete repertoire and sang a song in honor of the newlyweds:

Part III: The Last Adventures

Ezcon berriyac
pozquidac daudé
eguin diralaco gaur
alcarren jabé
elizan.

(The newlyweds are very happy because today
in church they were joined together.)

The party ended with the greatest joy at midnight when everyone went home.

When the honeymoon was over Martin went back to his travels. He did not stop; he would come and go between Spain and France without being able to rest.

Catherine fervently wished that the war would come to an end and she tried to keep Martin at home.

"What more do you want?" she would say to him. "Don't you already have enough money? Why risk your life any more?"

"But I'm not risking my life," Martin would answer.

But it was not true; he was ambitious, loved danger, and had a blind faith in his destiny. Being settled down irritated him.

Martin and Bautista would leave the two women alone and go off to Spain. One year after being married Catherine had a son whom they called Joseph Michael because Martin remembered old Tellagorri's advice.

Chapter II

In Which the "Breaking-Up" Is Begun

WITH THE PROCLAMATION OF the monarchy in Spain the ice began to melt in the Carlist camp.

The battle of Lacar, foolishly lost by the regular army in the presence of the new king, was encouraging to the Carlists; but in spite of the victory and the spoils, the Pretender's cause was deteriorating.

The battle of Lacar only served to enrich the repertory of war songs with a ballad that, rather than for soldiers, seemed to have been written for the female chorus of a musical comedy, and went like this:

> *In Lacar, my boy,*
> *you very nearly took a fall;*
> *if Charles kicks you with his boot,*
> *he'll send you to Paris*
> *like a rubber ball.*

It was difficult, when listening to this song, not to picture several chorus girls voluptuously vibrating their hips.

The Carlists were already talking of treason. With the failure of the siege of Irun and the retreat of the pretender Charles, Navarrese and Basque priests began to doubt the triumph of the cause. With the Saguntum proclamation distrust spread everywhere.

"They're cousins and they've come to an agreement," the distrustful, who were legion, would say.

Some, who had heard about a certain Alphonse, the brother of Charles, thought that this Alphonse had become king.

The ambitious villagers could see that all the upper classes were favorably disposed toward the liberal monarchy.

Alphonse's generals, after having gained all they could and having been promoted as high as possible, found that it was foolish to continue the war any longer; they had put an end to the republic, which certainly, because it was inept, deserved to be ended; the new government saw them as conquerors, peacemakers and heroes. What more could they want?

The "Breaking-up" was beginning in the Carlist camp. One could now walk along the roads without being attacked; Carlism continued, by dint of inertia, weakly defended and even more weakly attacked. Money was really the only weapon that was being brandished.

Martin, seeing that it was no problem to travel the roads, took his small coach and headed for Urbia one winter morning.

Not a sound could be heard from any of the strongholds; the Carlist trenches were silent; neither a gunshot nor a cloud of smoke penetrated the air. Snow covered the countryside with its white shroud under the cloudy, gray sky.

On both sides of the road to Urbia one could see crumbling country houses, façades with their windows covered up, stuffed with straw, trees with broken branches, trenches and parapets everywhere.

Martin entered Urbia. Catherine's house was in ruins, with the roof pierced by shells, the doors and windows firmly secured. The beautiful big house was a sorry sight; in the desolate garden the lilac trees displayed their broken branches, and one of the largest branches, from a magnificent, stripped linden tree, was hanging to the ground. The climbing rosebushes, once so luxuriant, were now withered.

Martin went up his street to see the house in which he was born.

The school was locked; through the dirty windows one could see the posters with large letters and the maps hanging on the walls. Near Zalacaín's house there was a wooden beam from which a bell was suspended.

"What's that for?" he asked a beggar who was going from door to door. It was for the lookout. Whenever he would notice a powder flash he would ring the bell to warn the people below.

Martin entered the Zalacaín house. There was no roof; only a corner of the old kitchen still had a covering. Under this ceiling, among the debris, sat a man writing and there was a little boy busy watching several cooking pots.

"Who lives here?" asked Martin.

"I do," a voice responded.

Martin was astonished. It was the foreigner. When they saw each other they shook hands affectionately.

"The talk you caused in Estella!" said the foreigner. "What a marvelous stroke that was! How did you fellows get away?"

Martin told the story of his escape and the journalist took notes.

"I can do a great story on this," he said.

Then they talked about the war.

"Poor country!" said the foreigner. "How much brutality! How much absurdity! Do you remember poor Haussonville, whom we met in Estella?"

"Yes."

"He was shot to death. And how about the bugler from Lasala and Praschcu, who were among those pursuing us near Hernani?"

"Yes."

"The two of them had saved the rebel leader Monserrat from dying. Do you know who shot them?"

"You mean they were shot?"

"Yes; the same Monserrat, in Ormaiztegui."

"Poor guys!"

"You must have known another man, named Anchusa, from the Priest's band..."

"Yes; I knew him."

"Lizarraga had him shot. And the soapmaker, the Priest's lieutenant..."

"They killed him too?"

"Him too. The Priest owed the only victory he won in Usurbil to the soapmaker when they defended a hermitage against the liberals; but he was jealous of him and he also believed that he was plotting against him, and he had him shot."

"If things go on like this we won't have anyone left."

"Fortunately, the 'breaking-up' has already begun, according to what the villagers say," replied the foreigner. "And what brings you here?"

Martin told him he was from Urbia, as was his wife, and he recounted his adventures since the last time he had seen the foreigner. They ate together and in the afternoon they said goodbye.

"I still think we'll see each other again," said the foreigner.

"Who knows; it's very possible."

Chapter III

Where Martin Begins to Work for Glory

DURING THE SNOWFALL PERIOD an audacious general who came from far away attempted to surround the Carlists alongside the Pyrenees and, leaving Pamplona, he went up the Elizondo road; but when he saw the heights of Velate defended and securely held by the Carlists, he withdrew toward Eugui and then went along the Olaberri pass, near the border, through forests and on very rough paths; and with the soldiers getting lost in the forests, after two days and three nights they reached Baztan.

They had acted very indiscreetly; but that general was lucky because if the terrible snowfall which fell the day after they were in Elizondo had come sooner, half the troops would have been buried in it.

The general requested provisions from France and, thanks to the aid of the neighboring country, he was able to feed his men and set up living quarters. Martin and Bautista were connected with a Bayonne firm and they took their wagons to Añoa.

Añoa is a half mile or so from the border, where the Dancharinea Spanish customs bureau is located.

That day a number of people from the French border appeared in Añoa. The road was crowded with long, narrow, two-wheeled carts and stage-coaches that were carrying to the Baztan valley for the troops bundles of shoes, bags of bread, boxes of hardtack from Bordeaux, matweed for beds and barrels of wine and whiskey.

The road was impassable and full of mud. Besides all those goods under convoy consigned to the army, there were other coaches crammed with goods that some Bayonne merchants were conveying to see if they could sell them at retail.

Also, near the bridge over the Ugarona Stream there were several liquor vendors with their baskets, bottles and other stuff.

Martin and his wife and Bautista and his approached Añoa and got rooms at the inn. Catherine wanted to see if she could find out anything about her brother.

At the inn they asked a boy, a Carlist deserter, but he could not tell them anything about Charles Ohando.

"If he isn't in Peñaplata, he's probably on his way to Burguete," he told them.

Martin and Bautista were standing by the door of the inn when Briones, Rosie's brother, passed by, wrapped in his overcoat. He greeted Martin very affectionately and went into the inn. He was wearing a major's uniform with gilded cordons which are worn by aides to generals.

"I have told my general a lot about you," he said to Martin.

"Really?"

"Yes, indeed. He would like very much to meet you. I've related your adventures to him. Would you like to come to say hello to him? I have a horse over there that belongs to my orderly."

"Where is the general?"

"In Elizondo. Coming?"

"Let's go."

Martin informed his wife that he was going to Elizondo; Briones and Zalacaín mounted and, chatting about many things, they arrived at that town, the center of the Baztan valley. The general was staying at a palatial residence on the square; two officers were conversing at the door.

Briones brought Martin to the general's room. The general, seated at a table on which were plans and papers, was smoking a cigar and debating with several people.

Briones introduced Martin and after shaking his hand, the general said to him abruptly:

"Briones has told me your adventures. I congratulate you."

"Thank you, sir."

"Are you familiar with all this border area around the Baztan valley?"

"Yes, like the back of my hand. I don't think there can be anyone else who knows it as well."

"Do you know the roads and paths?"

"There are only paths."

"Is there a trail that goes up to Peñaplata alongside Zugarramurdi?"

"There is."

"Can the horses get up?"

"Yes, easily."

The general debated with Briones and with the other aide. He had had the plan of blockading the border and preventing the retreat to France of the main body of the Carlist army, but it was impossible.

"You, what are your political leanings?" the general suddenly asked Martin.

"I've worked for the Carlists, but basically I think I'm a liberal."

"Would you like to serve as guide for the column that will go up to Peñaplata tomorrow?"

"I have no objection."

The general got up from the chair in which he was sitting and went with Zalacaín to one of the balconies.

"I believe," he told him, "that at the present time I am the most influential man in Spain. What do you want to be? Don't you have ambitions?"

"At the present time I am rather wealthy and so is my wife…"

"Where are you from?"

"Urbia."

"Do you want us to appoint you mayor of that town?"

Martin pondered.

"Yes, I'd like that," he said.

"Well, you can count on it. Tomorrow morning we must be here."

"Are troops going to go through Zugarramurdi?"

"Yes."

"I'll wait for them on the road, near the heights of Maya."

Martin said goodbye to the general and to Briones and he returned to Añoa to calm his wife. He related his conversation with the general to Bautista; Bautista told it to his wife and she to Catherine.

At midnight Martin was getting ready to mount his horse when Catherine appeared with her baby in her arms.

"Martin! Martin!" she said sobbing. "I've been told that you want to go with the army up to Peñaplata."

"Me?"

"Yes."

"It's true. And does that frighten you?"

"Don't go. They'll kill you, Martin. Don't go! For our son's sake! For my sake!"

"Bah! Don't be silly! What can you fear? If I've been alone other times, what can happen to me going with so many people?"

"Yes, but don't go now, Martin. The war is going to be over very soon. Don't let something happen to you at the end."

"I've made a promise. I have to go."

"Oh, Martin!" sobbed Catherine. "You mean everything to me; I have no father, no mother, nor do I have a brother, because the love I could have for him I have given to you and your son. Don't leave me a widow, Martin."

"Don't worry. Calm down. My life is not in danger, but I have to go. I've given my word…"

"For your son's sake…"

"Yes, for my son's sake too… When he grows up I don't want anyone to be able to say about him: 'This is the son of Zalacaín, who gave his word and did not keep it because he was afraid.' No, if they say anything, let them say: 'This is Michael Zalacaín, the son of Martin Zalacaín, as brave as his father… No. Braver even than his father!'"

And Martin, with his words, was able to encourage his wife; he caressed his son, who was smiling at him from his mother's lap; he embraced her and, mounting his horse, he disappeared down the Elizondo road.

Chapter IV

The Battle Near Mt. Aquelarre

MARTIN REACHED THE HEIGHTS of Maya, went up the road a little and saw the troops coming. He joined Briones and they both went to the head of the column.

When they got to Zugarramurdi it was beginning to grow light. Above the town the mountain tops, white and shiny because of the rain, were glistening in the early rays of the sun.

From this whiteness of the rocks came the name of Mt. Arrizurri (white stone) in Basque and *Peñaplata* in Spanish.

Martin took the trail that borders a torrent. A layer of wet clay was covering the road along which the horses and men were sliding. No sooner did the trail reach the ravine, filled with thickets and rotted tree trunks, than it left it again. The soldiers were falling down on this slippery terrain. At a certain height the torrent came to a steep cliff over which the sparkling water rushed to the bottom, which was full of thickets.

Martin and Briones were conversing amicably while riding along on their horses. Martin congratulated Briones for his promotions.

"Yes, I'm not unhappy," said the major; "but you, friend Zalacaín, are the one who's making it to the top fast; if in the coming years, with things going like this, you progress as much as you have in the last five years, you'll be able to go as high as you want."

"Would you believe that I hardly have any ambitions any more?"

"You don't?"

"No. Obviously it was the obstacles that gave me courage and strength, seeing that everyone was getting in my way to keep me back. If I wanted to live, an obstacle would pop up; if I loved a woman and she loved me, another obstacle. Now I have no obstacles and I don't know what to do. I'm going to have to invent other pursuits and other worries for myself."

"You are restlessness personified, Martin," said Briones.

"What do you expect? I grew up wild like the grass and I need action, continuous action. I often think that the day will come when men will be able to make use of the passions of others for something good."

"Are you a dreamer too?"

"That too."

"The truth is that you're a colorful fellow, friend Zalacaín."

"But most men are like me."

"Oh, no! Most of us are calm, quiet, a little languid."

"Well, I'm alive and active, that's for sure; but the very life that I can't use stays inside me and rots. You know, I just wish that everything could live, that everything could begin to move, not leaving anything standing still, pushing everything into motion—men, women, business, machines, mines—nothing still, nothing motionless."

"Strange ideas," murmured Briones.

The road came to an end and the paths began to divide and subdivide, scaling the heights.

When they reached this point Martin advised Briones that it would be a good idea for his troops to be prepared, since at the end of these paths they would be in open territory without the protection of any trees.

Briones ordered the marksmen of the vanguard to have their guns ready and to slowly move forward in guerrilla fashion.

"While some go this way," Martin said to Briones, "the others can go up along the opposite side. Up there is a big open space. If the Carlists set up a defense behind the rocks they'll massacre us."

Briones informed the general of what Martin had said and the general ordered half a battalion to go where the guide had indicated. As long as they did not hear shots from the main body of the forces they should not attack.

Zalacaín and Briones dismounted, took a path and for a couple hours they gradually encircled the mountain, going through ferns.

"Around here, at an open space of the mountain where there is a kind of little square formed by beech trees," said Martin, "the Carlists probably have sentinels; if not, we can climb at that point to the heights of Peña-plata with no difficulty."

When they approached the place Martin had indicated they heard a voice singing. Startled, they began to slow down their pace as they drew near.

"Do you suppose it's the witches?" said Martin.

"Why the witches?" asked Briones.

"Don't you know that these are the mountains of the witches? That one is Aquelarre," replied Martin.

"Aquelarre? You mean there is one?"

"Yes."

"And does that name mean something in Basque?"

"Aquelarre?... Yes, it means 'Meadow of the Buck.'"

"Can the buck be the devil?"

"Probably."

It was not the witches who were singing the song but a lad who, with ten or twelve others, was keeping warm by a campfire.

One was singing liberal and Carlist songs and the others would join in the chorus.

The first shots had not yet been heard, and Briones and his men waited stretched out between the thickets.

Martin felt a pang of remorse when he thought that those happy young men had only a few more minutes to live.

The signal was not long in coming, and it was not just one shot but a series of concealed volleys.

"Fire!" shouted Briones.

Three or four of the singers fell to the ground and the others, leaping between crags, began to flee and shoot.

The action was spreading; it had to be fierce, judging by the sound of the gunfire. Briones, his troops and Martin climbed the mountain with great difficulty. When they reached the heights, the Carlists, caught in a cross fire, retreated.

The extensive open space of the mountain was strewn with wounded and dead bodies. They were being picked up and put on stretchers. And the action continued; but soon an army column was closing in from another side of the mountain and the Carlists were running away helter-skelter toward France.

Chapter V

Where Modern History
Repeats Ancient History

MARTIN AND CATHERINE WENT in their little wagon to Saint-Jean Pied de Port. The entire main body of the Carlist army, in its retreat from Spain, was entering through the ravine of Roncesvalles and through Valcarlos. A number of merchants had gone down there, like vultures hovering over dead flesh, and were buying beautiful horses for ten to twelve dollars, swords, guns and clothes at extremely low prices.

It was rather repugnant to watch this exploitation, and Martin, feeling patriotic, spoke of the greed and baseness of the French. A Bayonne ragman told him that business is business and that everyone took what advantage he could.

Martin refused to discuss the matter. He and Catherine asked several Carlists from Urbia about Ohando, and one of them indicated that Charles, with Lefty, had left Burguete very late because he was very ill.

Not worrying about whether it was wise or not, Martin took his small coach along the Arneguy road; they went through that little town which has two districts, one Spanish and one French, on the banks of a stream, and they continued on to Valcarlos.

Catherine was horrified when she saw that spectacle. The narrow road was a field of desolation. Houses set on fire still smoldering, broken trees, trenches, the ground covered with war supplies—wagon boxes, artillery straps, bent bayonets, brass musical instruments crushed by carts.

Lying in the ditch at the side of the road was a half-nude corpse, with no boots, whose head was covered with fern leaves; mud was staining his face.

A cloud of crows was moving forward through the gray air following that dismal army to devour its remains.

Martin, mindful of Catherine's reaction, wisely turned around and went back to the French district of Arneguy. They entered the inn. The foreigner was there.

"Didn't I tell you we'd see each other again?" said the latter.

"Yes. That's right."

Martin introduced the journalist to his wife and the three together waited for the last soldiers to arrive.

At nightfall, in a group of six or seven men, Charles Ohando and Lefty appeared.

Catherine went toward her brother with open arms.

"Charles! Charles!" she shouted.

Ohando was dumbfounded when he saw her; then, with a gesture of anger and scorn he added:

"Get out of here. Slut! You have disgraced us!"

And in his brutishness he spat in Catherine's face.

Martin, blinded with rage, jumped on Charles like a tiger and grabbed hold of his neck.

"Scum! Coward!" he roared. "This very minute you are going to ask your sister to forgive you."

"Let go! Let go!" exclaimed Charles, choking.

"On your knees!"

"For God's sake, Martin, let him go!" shouted Catherine. "Let him go!"

"No, because he's a miserable, cowardly scum, and he's going to ask you to forgive him on his knees."

"No!" exclaimed Ohando.

"Yes!" and Martin dragged him by the neck through the mud to where Catherine was standing.

"Don't be cruel!" cried out the foreigner. "Let him go."

"Help, Lefty! Help!" Charles yelled in a stifled voice.

Then, before anyone could prevent it, Lefty, from the corner of the inn, raised his gun and took aim; there was the sound of a gunshot and Martin, wounded in the back, staggered, let go of Ohando, and fell to the ground.

Charles got up and kept looking at his opponent. Catherine threw herself over her husband's body and tried to raise him. It was useless.

Martin took his wife's hand and with his last ounce of strength raised it to his lips.

"Goodbye!" he murmured weakly. His eyes got misty and he died.

In the distance a warlike bugle sound was vibrating through the air of Roncesvalles.

Those mountains had trembled like that when Roland blew his horn.

And like that, about five hundred years before, Velche de Micolalde, a relative of the Ohandos, had also treacherously murdered Martin Lopez Zalacaín.

Catherine fainted beside her husband's dead body. The foreigner and some people from the inn attended to her. Meanwhile, a few French policemen pursued Lefty, and seeing that he was not going to stop, they fired several shots until he fell wounded.

MARTIN'S BODY WAS TAKEN inside the inn and kept there all night encircled by candles. The house was not large enough to hold all the friends who came. The abbot of Roncesvalles and the priests of Arneguy, Valcarlos and Zaro assisted in the funeral service.

The burial took place in the morning. The day was clear and bright. The coffin was taken out and placed in the coach that had been sent from Saint-Jean Pied de Port. All the farmers from the Ohando settlement properties were there; they had walked from Urbia to attend the burial service. Briones, wearing his uniform, Bautista Urbide and Capistun the American presided over the funeral.

And the women were crying.

"As great as he was," they were saying. "Poor fellow! Who would have thought that we, who have known him since he was a little boy, would have to attend his funeral!"

The cortege took the road to Zaro and there the sad ceremony came to an end.

Months later, Charles Ohando entered St. Ignatius of Loyola; Lefty was in the hospital where they amputated his leg, and then he was sent to a French prison; and Catherine and her child went to Zaro to live near Ignacia and Bautista.

Chapter VI

The Three Roses of the Zaro Cemetery

THE LITTLE TOWN OF Zaro is very small and is situated on a hill. To get to it one takes a road which is very low in some parts and over which leafy shrubs form a tunnel in the summertime.

At the entrance to Zaro, as in other French-Basque towns, there is a huge wooden cross which is very high and painted red, with different things associated with the Passion of Christ: a rooster, the crown of thorns, the lance and the nails. These crude crosses, with stars and hearts engraved in black, lend a gloomy, tragic aspect to Basque towns.

On top of the hill where Zaro is located, in the middle of a long, narrow little square rises a large, bushy walnut tree with a stone bench encircling its thick trunk.

One of the houses that make up the square is big, has a spacious porch, projecting eaves and several windows covered by green blinds. On the coat of arms which is displayed on the arch over the entrance, one can read the date of the construction of the house and several words written in Latin indicating who built it:

Bacalereus, presbiterus Urbide,
hoc domicilium fecit in lapide.

At one end of the small square is the humble little church with an atrium, belfry, and slate roof.

The cemetery extends around the church, separated from it by a low wall.

In Zaro there is always complete silence, almost solely interrupted by the broken sound of the church clock which strikes the hours melancholically with a weeping ring.

On the sundial of the tower of another Basque town, in Urruña, this bleak inscription is written: *"Vulnerant omnes; ultima, necat"* ("They all wound; the last one kills"). The bleak inscription could better still have been written on the clock of the Zaro tower.

In springtime different colored rosebushes—red, yellow, and white lilies with a gloomy appearance blossom between the stone crosses in the cemetery around the church.

From this cemetery one can see a very extensive valley, a pleasant, rural landscape. The feeble sounds of life in the town scarcely disturb the heavy silence that reigns in the cemetery.

From time to ti me one hears the squeaking of a door, the tinkling of cowbells, the voice of a little boy, the buzzing of bumblebees…, and from time to time one also hears the sound of a clock's bell-clapper, the voice of somber, submissive death, which sadly echoes through the valley.

The silence that follows this sinister bell-ringing seems like a tender caress.

As a protest against eternal life, in that very cemetery weeds grow vigorously, spread their hardy stems over the ground and lend a pungent odor to the twilight hours after the sun sets; birds chirp in a noisy gabble and roosters bravely crow as in defiance.

From there one can view an extensive panorama of smooth lines, bright verdure, with no austere rocks, somber thickets or anything harsh and wild. Small, white villages sleep over farms; narrow carts creak along the roads; farmers with their oxen work in the fields, and the fertile, moist land rests under the broad smile of the sky and the immense compassion of the sun…

There is a tombstone in the Zaro cemetery, and written on the cross in black letters are the Basque words:

HERE LIES
MARTIN ZALACAÍN,
WHO DIED AT THE AGE OF 24,
29 FEBRUARY 1876

One summer afternoon, many, many years after the war, three little old ladies, dressed in black, were seen entering the Zaro cemetery on the same day.

One of them was Linda; she went up to Zalacaín's grave and left a dark rose on it; the other lady was Miss Briones and she placed a red rose on the grave. Catherine, who would go to the cemetery every day, saw the two roses on her husband's tombstone and respected them, and she put a white rose next to them.

And for a long time the three roses stayed fresh on Zalacaín's grave.

Chapter VII

Epitaphs

THIS IS THE EPITAPH that the poet Echehun de Zugarramurdi improvised for the tomb of Zalacaín the Adventurer:

Lur santu onetan dago
Martin Zalacaín ló.
Eriotzac hill zuen
bazan salvatucó.
Eliz aldeco itzalac
gorde du beticó
bere icena dedin,
honratu gaur gueró,
aurrena Euscal Errien,
gloriya izatecó.

(*In this holy ground Martin Zalacaín is sleeping. Death struck him down, but he did attain salvation. In the adjoining presbyterium his name is kept forever, first of all for the honor of the Basque country and secondly for his own glory.*)

And the young Navarrese poet, Juan de Navascues, glossed the epitaph of the poet Echehun de Zugarramurdi in this ten-line stanza:

Martin Zalacaín, the strong,
sleeps in this grave.
Death took vengeance on him
for being so bold and so brave.
The Basque retains the memory
of his warlike gentleness;
and although the Book of History
rejects his crude name,
You, traveler of his people,
humble yourself before his fame!

About the Translator

JAMES P. DIENDL RECEIVED his B.A. and M.A. degrees from the Ohio State University. His major course of study is in Spanish with a specialty in Golden Age literature. Mr. Diendl's master's thesis is on the "Entremeses" of Cervantes. He has taught Spanish language and literature courses at the Ohio State University, Miami University in Oxford, Ohio, and at Mount Union College in Alliance, Ohio.

CPSIA information can be obtained
at www.ICGtesting.com
Printed in the USA
LVHW081626280420
654675LV00019B/2186